Weekly Reader Book Club presents

First Contact?

First Contact?

by

Hugh Walters

THOMAS NELSON INC.
Nashville / Camden / New York

Copyright © 1971, 1973 by Hugh Walters

All rights reserved under International and Pan-American Conventions. Published by Thomas Nelson Inc., Nashville, Tennessee. Manufactured in the United States of America.

First U.S. edition

Library of Congress Cataloging in Publication Data

Walters, Hugh.
    First contact?
    SUMMARY: Two spaceships on an exploratory voyage to Uranus come into contact with a being of superior intelligence from a distant world.
    [1. Science fiction.   2. Space flight—Fiction]
I. Title.
PZ7.W1715Fg3   [Fic]   73–10047
ISBN 0–8407–6320–4

Weekly Reader Book Club presents

First Contact?

1

For LONG MONTHS the two spaceships had hung seemingly motionless. In reality they were streaking along on their prearranged path toward one of the few planets that man had not yet visited—Uranus.

U-Alpha and U-Beta—that was what the ships were called—had been launched simultaneously from the vast spaceport at Cape Kennedy in Florida. The launching had been perfect, their trajectories accurate, and very soon the twin ships had settled down to the long voyage to the distant planet.

Morrison Kant, the young American astronaut, was in command of Alpha, while his friend, the Russian astronaut Serge Smyslov, commanded Beta. In overall command, in charge of the whole expedition, was the Englishman, Christopher J. Godfrey, the deputy director of the United Nations Exploration Agency.

Never before had UNEXA despatched two ships on the same voyage of exploration. Never before had two ships had such highly trained and efficient crews, every one of whom had made many space flights before. Chris Godfrey —the Admiral, as some of his companions were beginning to call him—was the most experienced interplanetary voyager of them all.

Chris had only recently been promoted to deputy director of UNEXA. Before that he had been the agency's number one pilot, having started his trips into space when he'd barely left school. His old friend Sir George Benson had retired the year before after many years as director of UNEXA and had been made a Life Peer in recognition of his outstanding services to science in general and space travel in particular.

It had been on Lord Benson's recommendation that Chris had been appointed deputy. The young man had accepted the post with mixed feelings. It was a great honor and a splendid tribute to him, but he didn't feel he wanted to be grounded yet. Only when Lord Benson had agreed to let him go on the next expedition—this one to Uranus—had Chris finally agreed to his promotion.

Of course his friends Morrey and Serge, together with that other close friend, the chief mechanic, Tony Hale, had been delighted, especially when they knew that he would share at least one more trip with them.

It would be hard when the time came for these four young men to stop working as a team. There were few places in the solar system which they had not visited together. The dangers they had faced had made them closer than brothers. Each, secretly, dreaded the time when Chris would have to remain on Earth. But now all four were speeding toward a planet that man had never visited before.

Why had UNEXA—never anxious to waste money—decided to send two ships on the expedition? The answer was simple. It wasn't merely to ensure that one, at least, returned safely from the hazards of space. It was because astronomers were puzzled and worried about strange happenings on that distant world. In the opinion of Earth's foremost scientists, it was vital to find out the cause of the mysterious radio signals that had started to come from Uranus. And so a full-scale, two-ship expedition had been despatched, manned by the best possible crews under the command of Chris Godfey.

Plans for such an undertaking had existed in a rough

8

form for some time. When, however, the agency had decided on the expedition as a matter of some urgency, the flight plans had been expanded and finished in record time. Precisely on schedule Alpha and Beta blasted off from their launching pads and climbed rapidly into the clear blue sky.

At first the two ships had gone into a parking orbit. Side by side they had circled the Earth while the final calculations were put through the computer. Then, together, they had broken orbit and had set out on their long journey.

There was a crew of four to each ship. In Alpha, besides Chris and Morrey, there were Norman Spier and Colin Johnson. These two astronauts, alike in their high degree of skill and training, were quite unlike physically. Norman was completely bald, which made him look older than he was, while Colin had a mass of long dark hair which, the others declared, added considerably to the rocket's payload!

Beta, of course, carried Serge and Tony the mechanic. The other two were Mervyn Williams, an excitable Welshman, and Robert Campbell, an Ulsterman with a Scottish name. Because Chris and his two crews had been specially selected and trained, they knew they could work as a closely knit team, though this didn't prevent them from teasing each other unmercifully.

However, there was no teasing, and no conversation of any kind, in the ships just now. Because the long journey would take many months, both the crews had been put into a state of hypothermia. This was a type of freezing especially developed for space travel. By this means the astronauts were literally frozen, only to be thawed out and returned to life when required.

Chris had been in the "ice box" on many occasions. It was painless and just like falling into a long sleep. Time meant nothing, and when he was restored to life, it was difficult to realize that so much time had elapsed. One minute he would be waiting for the hypothermia to begin. The next minute—or so it would seem—it would be all over, yet weeks, or perhaps months, would have passed.

Hypothermia had become a standard practice for all crews on long-distance voyages. It spared them the utter boredom of being confined in a small space for long periods, and it saved a considerable amount of payload in the way of food and water. At intervals during the flight, both crews were revived for short periods to allow them to make scientific observations and to carry out any necessary corrections to the flight path. One of the periods of activity was rapidly approaching.

In both Alpha and Beta the astronauts were in special compartments which they had christened "the fridge." The still figures lay strapped to couches without showing any signs of life. They would remain thus until the apparatus controlling the temperature was switched off. Then the temperature of the fridge would slowly rise, and life would seep back into them.

Within half an hour, the crew of U-Alpha had revived and shortly afterward the Beta crew reported by radio. The first task was always to inspect the ships carefully, both inside and out. This was to find any damage that might have been caused by meteorites since the last inspection. Though the chance of any serious damage was extremely remote, it was one they could not afford to take. Because of the double layer of the outer casing of each ship, the cosmic dust that abounds in space was no problem. The outer casing usually showed signs of a slight roughening. If anything larger than a grain of sand hit a ship, the outer skin might be penetrated, but the hole would be sealed instantly and automatically. Only a piece of space debris half an inch in diameter or larger could cause any serious damage.

"Your turn to do EVA," Chris said to Norman Spier.

He was referring to "extravehicular activity," as space walks outside the ship were officially called. The astronauts all liked the exhilarating experience of floating outside the ship, for the intense sense of freedom they felt was only matched by their wonder at the view of space. His bald head glistening with pleasure, Norman began the process of putting on his suit. Chris helped him, while Morrey and Colin Johnson began the inspection of the ship's interior.

A few miles away in Beta, Serge Smyslov had allocated EVA duty to Mervyn Williams—to the disgust of Bob Campbell.

"Sure, it's me turn to take a walk outside," Bob protested.

"Hark at him, now," Mervyn replied. "It's a short memory that he has. Was it not this man who did a jig on the casing last time?"

"Turn it in, you two." Serge laughed. He knew that nothing he could say would stop the perpetual arguments between these two members of his crew, who were the greatest of friends.

So Mervyn, too, put on his space suit and life-support pack, ready for his excursion outside.

"We're ready," Serge told Chris over the radio. "Mervyn is on his way out now."

"Tell that Welsh wizard not to do anything foolish," the voice of Chris came back. He knew that often, in the exhilaration of floating free in boundless space, even the most restrained of astronauts sometimes did queer things. Serge quickly checked Mervyn's suit and gave the thumbs-up sign, indicating that he could go through the airlock. Mervyn waved back and then clumped over toward the airlock hatch, the magnetic soles of his shoes clanging on the cabin's steel floor. He opened the door of the small compartment that would only admit one man at a time. Serge closed the door behind him and tightened the handle. A few seconds later a red light winked over the door. This meant that the outer door was open and the astronaut was gazing out into space.

It was now that the poet in the Welshman took over.

"Beautiful it is, like a great black mantle with diamonds sewn all over," Williams intoned over his helmet radio.

"He's off," sighed Tony Hale, who was just about to squeeze through a hatch to inspect the fuel-tank compartment. "He'll be bursting into song any minute."

"Get on with the job, Mervyn," Serge ordered. "You can describe the scenery later."

"Have you no feeling in your soul, man?" came the aggrieved voice of Mervyn. "Or has that Irish layabout put you up to it?"

Robert, the Ulsterman, was about to send a forceful reply back, but Serge waved him away from the microphone.

Outside, Mervyn clipped his safety line to one of the metal loops in the outer casing. This was a standard practice when astronauts were engaged on EVA unless, of course, they carried their jet guns with them. However, for a routine examination for meteor damage, the crewman would clamber over the ship with the help of his magnetic boots.

Tearing his gaze away from the star-studded heavens, Mervyn began the task in hand. Carefully he examined every square foot of the outer casing, and, apart from the usual abrasions caused by space dust, the ship appeared to be undamaged. At one point he did notice a small, black-edged hole, but this had been sealed automatically by the fluid between the outer and inner cases.

Inside Beta, Tony and Robert had also completed their examination, so Serge was able to radio to Chris that his ship was undamaged.

The next job was for the two ships to get a radar fix on each other, for in their flight plan they were not to be allowed to drift more than eighteen miles apart. Neither must they approach each other nearer than five miles. Perhaps it was an unconscious admission of the utter loneliness of space that the crews preferred to ride as closely as possible.

"Twenty-five miles, Admiral," Morrey told Chris in Alpha. So they were too far apart.

"All right. Close in to eight miles," Chris ordered.

This would mean a short burst from one of the lateral rockets that lay in a ring round the ship. When Alpha and Beta were the desired distance apart, a further short burst from another lateral would stop any further drift together.

"We're coming in," Morrey radioed over to Serge. "Will you keep track?"

The Russian acknowledged, and said he'd watch the radar himself. In Alpha, Morrey pressed one of a panel of firing buttons, and a slight tremor passed through the ship. At least there was nothing wrong with that particular rocket.

"Twenty-one. Twenty. Nineteen," Serge called into the microphone, his eyes glued on to the radar and the range finder.

"I can see the little darlin'," Robert called out. He'd been peering through one of the observation windows, and he could see a speck of light that had moved and grown appreciably larger. Yes, Alpha was closing in, and a few minutes later they were riding together just over eight miles apart. Morrey had given a short blast to kill the drift, and now the two ships appeared to hang motionless, with infinite space around them.

Though some eight miles separated Alpha and Beta, such was the clarity of the void between them that they seemed less than a quarter of that distance apart. Tony declared that he could see the bald head of Norman Spier shining from the window of the other ship.

"I'm hungry," announced Colin Johnson. "When do we break to eat?"

"I was just going to order a meal break," Chris told

him. "Are you hungry, too, in Beta?"

A chorus of Yeses came over the radio, so "the Admiral" gave the promised command.

Though the crews didn't require food or water during the long periods when they were frozen, they needed to eat and drink very soon after being revived. While Colin was raiding the food stores in Alpha, Tony was doing the same thing in her sister ship. Though the snacks were not like the food on Earth, because they had to be eaten under conditions of weightlessness, they were appetizing and satisfying. All the astronauts had long since become used to chewing strange-looking cubes of food which tasted a great deal better than they looked. The liquids they had to suck from plastic containers, for if left free, any liquid would break up into countless globules, because of the lack of gravity to hold it together.

It was during this lunch break that Morrey asked Chris if it wouldn't be a good idea to reshuffle the crews. Perhaps two of the Alpha crew could exchange with two Beta men. At least it would bring some variety into what could be a long, tedious voyage.

"I'll think about it if we get too fed up with each other's company," Chris promised with a smile. "But we can't waste jet power crossing between ships just for social calls."

Mealtime over, the two crews set about their next task of plotting their position against the various stars. This information, sent back to Cape Kennedy, would enable the computer to work out their exact course and speed. Then it would be seen if any correction of their flight path was needed. Chris collected all the data from his companions and read the figures over the radio.

14

2

At the special invitation of Sir Billy Gillanders, the new director, his predecessor had come to the Cape Kennedy Control. Lord Benson was delighted at this opportunity to meet some of his former colleagues again. Before his retirement, Lord Benson had organized and directed fantastic spaceflights. This present undertaking to Uranus was the first that had been the responsibility of his successor.

George Benson had every confidence in the tall Australian. There was one thing Benson was resolved never to do —to appear as if he still wanted to be in charge. "Breathing down Billy's neck," he'd called it. He'd only come to the Cape in response to a very definite and pressing invitation from his friend.

"I thought you would like to come here at this time," Sir Billy explained. "The crews should be having a period of activity, and I guess you'd like to have a word with them."

Lord Benson was deeply touched. There was nothing he would like more than to speak to Chris and the others. Chris had known "Uncle George" since his schooldays.

Benson also knew Tony, Morrey, and Serge very well, and he had sent them, together with Chris, on many dangerous voyages. Often their lives had depended on some decision of his, and it was with mixed feelings of relief and sadness that he realized the responsibility had now passed to another.

"How's the flight going?" he asked, and Sir Billy reeled

15

off a string of technical details at which the former director nodded approvingly.

"Not a hitch, then," he said with satisfaction. "And when are they due to fly past the target?"

"In another thirty-one days."

"Will they go into orbit?"

"Undoubtedly unless it's unsafe to do so or unless they find the cause of the radio signals beforehand," Sir Billy answered.

"Ah—yes, those radio signals," breathed Lord Benson. "Tell me more about them, Billy."

"Well, they started coming in over a year ago," Gillanders said. "At first they were very faint, and it was as much as Jodrell Bank could do to pick them up and locate the source. They're coming from a point on Uranus all right, and they're getting stronger all the time. Now they are ten times as strong as when we first picked them up."

"What are they like?" asked Benson.

"Come over here and listen to this recording," Sir Billy invited him.

The two men went over to a soundproof room leading from the main hall of the control center. Sir Billy closed the door behind them, blotting out every sound from the hall. He strode over to some electrical apparatus, made a few adjustments, and then switched on. Lord Benson listened intently.

At first there was nothing but the sound of static. Then came a low whistle, rising steadily in pitch until it was almost inaudible. After that the pitch fell steadily until the whistle disappeared, leaving only static coming from the tape. After an interval of nearly a quarter of a minute the low whistle was heard again, and the process was repeated.

"The complete cycle takes ninety-four seconds precisely," the director told his friend, "and it doesn't vary."

He switched off the tape machine and turned to the other.

"What do you make of it?" he asked.

Benson was very thoughtful.

"I've certainly never heard anything like it before," he admitted. "What about the wave pattern?"

"That's unique, too," Sir Billy said.

He went to a drawer and took out a roll of paper. Along it ran the wavering line of the recorder. Lord Benson bent over it and ran a few yards through his hands. He was silent for some time. Then he handed the roll back to his friend.

"Billy, that could be artificial," he said gravely.

"That's what I think," Gillanders agreed. "In fact that's the general opinion."

"And there's no doubt where it's coming from?"

"None whatsoever. It's coming from Uranus all right. And its overall fluctuation coincides with the planet's period of rotation—ten and three-quarter hours."

Uranus was discovered in 1781 by Sir William Herschel, who became the King's Astronomer a year later. It circles the Sun at an average distance of no less than 1,782,000,000 miles. This means that light—or radio signals—would take some two and three quarter hours to travel between Uranus and Earth. So the strange signals that had been detected had been winging their way across space for that length of time.

Uranus is somewhat larger than our home planet, having a diameter of 32,000 miles. Lord Benson frowned slightly as he recalled that very little else was known about it, except that its atmosphere seemed to consist mainly of a gas called methane and that the temperature was very low indeed.

What the planet itself was like could only be a matter of conjecture, for no probes had been sent to it so far. No

17

doubt UNEXA had Uranus on its list for unmanned exploration at an early date, but these mysterious signals had upset the program. Their cause had to be discovered. Hence the two-ship expedition into this unknown part of the solar system.

"What are the flight plans?" Lord Benson asked after a lengthy pause.

"Provisionally, Alpha will dip into the atmosphere and try to pinpoint the source and find out what it is that is transmitting," Sir Billy replied. "Meanwhile, Beta will continue to orbit the planet as a backup."

"Any plans for landing?"

"None, but of course Chris has complete discretion. As you know, we can't tell what the surface is like or if it will be possible to put a ship down on it. Chris won't risk it unless he thinks it's vital to do so."

"Well, I'd better send my message," Lord Benson said, smiling. "Otherwise I'll never get a reply. What's the time lag?"

"A hundred and ten minutes." So it would take a message nearly two hours to reach the spaceships and another two hours to get a reply. The two men moved over to a microphone and a technician linked it to the powerful transmitter. Billy passed the mike to his former chief.

Lord Benson took it, wondering what he should say. Because of the time lag, no conversation was possible and anything he said might sound rather stiff, as if he were making a statement.

"Hello, Chris, and all of you," he began, "I don't suppose you expected to hear from this old crock. Billy has invited me to spend a few hours down at the Cape, and I understand you're having a period of activity. I'm going to hang on here until your reports come through, though I understand you're smack on target."

Lord Benson then went on to give a personal message

18

to each of the astronauts, though he didn't know Spier, Johnson, Williams, and Campbell as intimately as he did the other four. When he'd finished, he handed the microphone to Sir Billy, who added his own comments. It was strange to think that their words wouldn't reach Alpha and Beta for nearly two hours. Before Chris's reply came back there would be time to have a look round the spaceport as well as for the two friends to enjoy a leisurely meal. So this is just what they did.

"We ought to be getting back to Control," Billy Gillanders said at last, glancing at his watch:

"I've been keeping my eye on the time, too," said Lord Benson.

As they reached the long instrument-packed room, Chris's voice was sounding from a loudspeaker. Even though he was stringing off masses of technical information in a monotone, Benson was delighted to hear it. It reminded him of the many occasions when he himself had had communications with the astronaut on which many lives had depended. This was just routine stuff that Chris was reading out, but sometimes it had been different. Benson shuddered slightly and forced his mind back to the present.

"Wonder what he'll think when he hears my voice," he mused.

"We should know any minute now," Gillanders answered with a glance at the large Control Room clock.

There was a pause in the incoming flow of data. For nearly a minute the loudspeaker was silent. Then Chris's voice burst out. Gone was the monotone. Even at that vast distance the listeners in Control could detect the surprise and pleasure that he felt.

"Uncle George, by all that's wonderful!" the voice said. "It's grand to hear from you again. The rest of the fellows want to follow me at our mikes, so I won't be too long. Everything in the two ships is fine. We're all very fit and happy, thanks to our long sleep. When we've cleared up this bit of a job about the radio signals, we'll hurry back. Then we must get together. I'll have a fair amount of leave due, so don't be too far away when we get back to the Cape. Here's Tony."

One after another the other members of the two crews spoke to Lord Benson. Soon the former director was speaking back to the crews, and an invitation for Chris to spend part of his leave with him was winging its way across space.

"Want to stay and hear the reply?" Sir Billy asked.

Lord Benson shook his head. He knew that if he waited the three and three quarter hours or so for Chris to answer his latest message, he'd be tempted to send another one. And so it would go on. Better for him to go now and not wear out his welcome.

"No, you can record it for me. But perhaps I'll be able to come again just before they reach target. Or maybe when they're on the way back."

"Come whenever you wish," Billy said. "I'll get some firm dates off you before you go."

After he'd seen his old friend away, Billy returned to study the data that had been coming in from the ships. The computer had already decided that no course correction was necessary, and both ships and crews seemed to be in good shape. Chris had reported, however, that the mysterious radio signals were very powerful from their present position. It was difficult to listen to them for long, for their eerie sounds had a curious effect on the crews. The sounds seemed to penetrate right into their brains, leaving them with painful headaches until the receiver was switched off.

Billy decided to check with his own staff, and though reception of the Uranus signals was still comparatively weak, two technicians had complained of splitting headaches after spells of duty. The problem would have to be passed over to the medical boys, Billy decided. He gave instructions for Control staff to be very careful about auditory monitoring of the Uranus signals. They were to listen in to the strange sounds no more than was necessary, and the work was to be done in the soundproof room by volunteers.

Meanwhile Sir Billy sent an order racing across space to his crews. They too were to take the utmost precautions when listening to the voice from Uranus. They were to keep the volume to a minimum and the duration no more than one cycle at a time. As he turned away from the microphone, the director looked serious. He'd never before heard of a radio signal that had such an uncomfortable effect on its audience.

Back in his office, Billy put phone calls through to Jodrell Bank, Singapore, the Philippines, and each of the other main listening stations. In each one the story was the same. Though the station managers were at first reluctant to mention it, and each had dismissed the matter as trivial, every one had had staff down with the same symptoms.

There could be no doubt about it. The signals from Uranus were having an uncomfortable effect on listeners on Earth and in the two spaceships. Fortunately the effect disappeared very quickly after the signals were cut off. But if they continued to increase in strength at the same rate that they had done since they were first detected, they might cause serious disturbance of terrestrial radio.

Billy ordered a careful examination of all the recordings that had been made, the research into the wave pattern was given top priority. He would not decide on the next step until he'd found out what it was that had this effect.

It seemed that it was going to be more important than anyone had at first realized that the menacing voice from Uranus should be explained.

3

CHRIS WAS SURPRISED and delighted when the voice of his old friend came through over the radio. So many times in the past Uncle George had passed on messages of hope and encouragement when things had been particularly sticky. It had always been a great comfort to talk to him and to know that he was at Control in times of crisis. Though he had retired, and Chris had equal confidence in Billy Gillanders, it gave him an extra sense of security to know that Uncle George was at the other end of that long, invisible link.

Not that there was any need for reassurance, Chris told himself. Everything had gone well on the expedition. The flight plan was being followed exactly. Thanks to hypothermia, the crew was fit and had not been bored by the long journey. Both ships had functioned faultlessly, and he was very proud of his space fleet.

It was only these wretched radio signals from their target that were a bit of a headache. He smiled to himself as he noticed that he had unconsciously used the right word. For the sounds from Uranus were certainly giving the crews an uncomfortable time if they were listened to for more than a few seconds. Every member of both crews was affected, Norman Spier perhaps worst of all.

"It's because you have no hair to protect that empty head of yours," Colin Johnson informed him.

"If that's so, you oughtn't to feel a thing," Norman snorted.

22

"Stop squabbling and go get the 'fridge' ready," said Morrey, grinning, for their period of activity would soon be over, and they would shortly have to undergo another spell in the freezer. The crews welcomed these interludes, for every time they woke their objective seemed to have leaped nearer. When they looked out of their observation windows, they could see that Uranus, instead of being a tiny point of light, was appearing as a small disk. Next time they defrosted, it would have grown appreciably larger.

The last message was exchanged with Control, the last data were transmitted. The two crews chatted with each other, and then Chris gave the order for them all to go to their hypothermia compartments. Even as they settled on their couches and adjusted the electrical connections about them, they exchanged jibes until Morrey and Serge switched on. Then they all fell silent, waiting to see if they could detect the onset of the deep sleep into which they would fall.

As usual, they couldn't. Before they knew it their vital processes had virtually ceased—just as the passage of time, for them, had stopped also. And so they lay motionless, while Alpha and Beta sped on toward the source of those frightening radio signals.

Chris opened his eyes. He knew at once that he'd just been aroused from hypothermia. A second before—or so it seemed—he'd been awaiting its onset. As usual, it had crept over him by stealth, and he still couldn't detect any break in his consciousness. He slid off his couch to look at his companions.

Morrey, Norman, and Colin still lay motionless, but the improving color of their flesh indicated the approaching return to life. He turned away, well satisfied. There was nothing he could do to help them. It was better if they awakened naturally. Was anyone awake in Beta? he wondered. He'd switch on and see if he could call one of the crew. Carefully he climbed down the hatch into the main cabin and clumped across toward the main radio. He flicked over the switch.

It took barely ten seconds for the apparatus to warm up, and Chris was just about to broadcast his reveille when the voice from Uranus filled the cabin. Chris held his ears in anguish as the sound rose higher. Even so he could hear the penetrating noise. Only when the signal had completed its cycle and momentarily died away was he able to take his hands from his ears and switch off the radio.

To say that he was staggered would be an understatement. He'd listened to the signals from Uranus before, of course, but on an entirely different wavelength from the one used for communication between the two ships. It seemed that Uranus had changed its radio frequency and was now obliterating any signals between Alpha and Beta.

Apart from the disastrous effect that lack of communication between the two ships would have, there was also a terribly disturbing possibility. Had the wavelength of the planet's broadcasts been deliberately changed by some intelligent agency? Chris couldn't recall a single instance of a natural radio source doing this. And it must be more than coincidence that their particular frequency had been selected.

The full horror of his deductions was just beginning to dawn on him when Norman Spier came clambering down from the fridge. He was visibly shaken.

"Chris," he burst out, "I heard that. I—I think it must have woken me."

Norman's face and bald head were usually a healthy, shining pink. Now he was looking quite pale, and Chris hastened to reassure him.

"You may have heard the voice, Norman," he said, "but you were due to wake up, as I've just done. You were probably conscious when I switched on. I don't think this ghastly noise can penetrate hypothermia. It hasn't affected Morrey or Colin."

"Maybe I'm more sensitive to it," Norman muttered, and then he grinned self-consciously. If this was so, he knew his friends would insist that it was solely due to his bald, unprotected cranium. Then he saw how worried Chris looked.

"It's blotting out our channel to Beta," the leader explained. Just then Colin and Morrey joined them, and Chris told them what had happened.

Colin Johnson was Alpha's radio expert, but he couldn't understand this intrusion of Uranus into their wavelength. Previously the planet's signals had been on short wave, whereas when speaking to each other the spaceships used V.H.F., for they would always be in "radio sight" of each other, and this conserved power.

"It's as if we've been monitored and our frequency discovered," Colin suggested uneasily.

"Rubbish," Morrey insisted. "That would imply an intelligence with advanced radio equipment on Uranus."

Colin shrugged his shoulders and asked his companions if any of them had a better explanation. And, of course, none of them had.

"How are we going to get through to Beta?" Norman asked. "We can't use the usual frequency."

"I can easily change that," said Colin, "but the difficulty will be letting them know. Their receiver will have to be changed to correspond."

They fell silent while they pondered this difficult problem. That the two ships should keep in constant radio contact was vital to the success of the expedition.

"I wonder if they have found the same?" wondered Morrey. "They will be puzzling how to get in touch with us."

"My guess is that, like us, they will try changing their wavelength," Colin ventured. "It will be a sheer fluke if we both hit on the same one."

As Morrey had guessed, the crew of Beta, now all fully conscious, had made the same alarming discovery. It was Tony who had suggested changing their frequency, but the same difficulty struck him.

"If only we could send them a letter to let them know our new wavelength," he said in an attempt to amuse his friends. And that gave him an idea.

"Hey, wait a bit!" Tony called. "How far away is Alpha?"

Serge went to the instrument panel and studied it.

"Roughly sixteen kilometers," he announced.

"What's that? Oh, divide by eight and multiply by five," muttered Tony. "Ah—ten miles. I could do it."

"Now what is the man on about?" demanded Mervyn.

"I've always wanted to cross to Alpha," Tony explained, "but Chris would never let us waste our jets. Surely he would agree under the circumstances. In any case, he can't stop me now we can't use the radio," Tony added ingenuously.

"No, but I can," Serge soon told him. However, there was merit in the mechanic's idea. If they could bring the two ships closer together, it would be possible for one of the crew to propel himself across space from one to the other, and so arrange the new wavelength. They discussed the possibility, and it was agreed to make the attempt.

"I'll go," Tony said. "It was my idea."

Mervyn and Robert also put forward their claims. Serge himself would have liked to do it, but his duty was plainly to remain with Beta. So he agreed Tony should make the trip.

"Get suited up," he ordered.

With the slightly envious help of the others, Tony

climbed into his space suit. Then, while he checked his jet guns, Serge fired a small lateral rocket to bring Beta nearer to her companion.

"Ye needn't come back," Robert told Tony. "It'll be a mercy not to look at your face for a while."

"Take you no notice of that Irishman," Mervyn advised. "It is his own face, indeed, that we could do without seeing."

"Won't you two ever stop arguing?" Serge sighed. "Have you decided on a suitable frequency, Tony?"

"No, I'll discuss it with Chris and Colin," Tony replied. "And, Serge, I think it would be as well to agree on a whole string of frequencies, don't you?"

There was a heavy silence in the cabin. Though no one spoke, everyone thought of the sinister radio signals. What Tony was suggesting was that it would be prudent to arrange a number of alternative frequencies in case the broadcast from the planet swamped their new wavelength. If it did, if the Uranus signals changed frequency with them, the implication would be frightening. Something or someone on the planet was determined to obstruct the undertaking. Furthermore, it must be monitoring the two ships' radios, and it must have the technical ability to broadcast on whatever wavelength was chosen.

"This is only assumption," Serge said sharply, guessing what the others were thinking. "We'll probably be all right if we change our wavelength. There is almost certainly some simple explanation of why Uranus is now using our frequency. I still can't think that these signals are anything but a hitherto unknown natural phenomenon."

"Sure, I hope the man is right," said Robert with a slight shudder.

"If you're going, you'd better start," Serge said quickly. Tony was all ready, his jet guns full, and he was looking forward to an exhilarating trip across space to Alpha.

"Try your helmet radio," said Serge.

Tony switched it on, but turned it off again immediately with a grimace.

"It's no use," he said. "Uranus is still calling."

It would be difficult to alter the frequency of the small transmitters that were built into the astronauts' space helmets and tuned to the ships' radio. When Tony stepped out into the void, he would be unable to communicate with his friends; he would be utterly on his own. But that didn't seem to deter him, and with his helmet finally in position he waved to his companions and stepped into the airlock. The signal light in the cabin indicated that the air in the lock had been extracted and that the outer door was now open.

Tony paused for a moment, looking out of the hatch. He was, perhaps, the least imaginative of all the members of the two crews, but even he was awed by the wonder of the diamond-littered space. Blazing away—so fiercely that he couldn't face it without bringing down the special vizor in his helmet—was the Sun. In every other direction was a profusion of stars, with the great band of the Milky Way predominating. Somewhere on the other side of the ship lay Uranus, the objective which was beginning to worry them so much.

But where was Alpha? Tony knew that in the incredible clarity of space he ought to see the spaceship even though she was so far away. He paused, studying the panorama of the heavens.

Ah! there she was! A point of light was slowly moving relative to the other glowing points. That would be Alpha without doubt. But it seemed so far away, that for a moment Tony experienced unaccustomed qualms. Now this wouldn't do, he told himself. He'd a job to do, and the safety of the two ships depended on it. He pushed himself gently away from the ship.

Carefully choosing the direction, he released a jet from his gun. It pointed away from Alpha so that he was thrust toward it. He mustn't use too much of the compressed gas just yet, for he had a long journey to go. With his own ship, Beta, seeming to move away from him, he had the impression that he was hanging, motionless, in space. Instead, he was moving across the void between the two ships.

His attention was focused mainly on the moving spot of light ahead. He kept his eyes on it as if it would vanish if he let it out of sight. Already it was assuming size and shape, and his own ship was shrinking. Soon he would be midway between the two vessels.

Under normal circumstances, there would have been a continuous exchange of chatter between himself and both crews. Tony loved the verbal fencing matches that concealed the astronauts' affection for each other and perhaps also their hopes and fears. He found it strange to have to observe an enforced radio silence because of the Uranus signals. It would be a relief to knock on the door of Alpha and announce he'd called for tea.

He hoped Chris and the others were expecting him. Though no radio communication was possible, he had little doubt that his EVA had been monitored by Alpha's radar. Chris would be watching his approach and had probably guessed its purpose. No doubt even now Colin Johnson was drawing up plans for the changes in radio frequencies.

Tony noticed that he was slightly off course. Never mind. It would be easy to correct his direction by another short squirt from his gun. He held it away from the direction he wanted to go and pressed the trigger.

Nothing happened. There was no stream of compressed gas shooting out of the gun's nozzle like the exhaust of a miniature rocket. Tony pressed the trigger again and again. Still no result. Worried, he held it close to his vizor to see what was wrong. It seemed all right, but it still obstinately refused to operate.

Had he been in the cabin, he could easily have corrected any fault in the gun's simple mechanism. But it was a different story out here in space. His gloved hands held the gun clumsily, and he had no tools. Even as he shook the gun desperately, hoping to free it, Tony could see that soon he would be moving farther away from Alpha instead of nearer to it.

And if that happened he would be truly lost in space, doomed to travel ever farther from his friends until his oxygen was exhausted, and he became an inanimate piece of space debris.

4

"Hey, what's happening out there?" Norman called.

He'd been watching the image of Beta on the radar screen and had seen a tiny body break away from it. Chris and the others crowded round the screen.

"We're going to have a visitor," Chris guessed. "I wonder what the idea is."

"That's easy," Colin replied loftily. "They can't send us a message by radio, so they're sending a postman."

"I wonder who it is and what he's coming for?" pondered Norman Spier.

"My guess is that it's to tell us about changing the radio frequencies," Morrey said. "It's a sure bet they've been thinking along the same lines that we have."

"But why send someone across space just to tell us that?" Norman asked. "It would have been quicker to tell us by radio."

"Fathead," bellowed Colin, and Norman, realizing how silly his remark had been, blushed all over his shining bald head.

"He's off course," Chris said suddenly. He'd been watching the tiny blip on the screen, and he could see that the astronaut, whoever he was, wasn't heading straight for Alpha. "He'll have to correct himself pretty soon."

They all watched the screen closely. There was no change in the Beta man's direction.

"What's he playing at?" Colin said. "He can see us, can't he?"

31

"He can see us all right," Chris told him. "We can see Beta, so Beta can see us."

"Then why doesn't he come straight to us?"

They continued to watch until the true explanation dawned on Chris.

"His gun's jammed!" he burst out. "It must be."

The horror of the situation dawned on them in a flash. The man they were watching would miss the target and continue past Alpha to be lost for ever in the limitless void. Only for a second did the crew remain frozen.

"I'm going after him," Chris snapped.

Normally there would have been an argument as to who should undertake this hazardous venture. But discussion would have wasted time—and every second was precious. While Colin examined the space gun, Morrey and Norman helped Chris into his suit. He was ready in record time, and he hurried to the airlock.

By now the envoy from Beta had passed beyond Alpha and was moving farther away every moment. There wasn't a second to lose. Chris sprang away from his ship and shot out a blast from his gun. He must overtake the unfortunate astronaut before he'd gone too far. Otherwise there wouldn't be enough power left in Chris's own gun to bring them both back safely.

With a sigh of relief Chris saw that he was overtaking the crewman. He could imagine the agony of mind that the other must be feeling at being lost in space. In such a situation there could only be one end—a slow death from oxygen starvation.

Chris gave himself another little nudge from his jet gun. He was now near enough to see that his quarry was fumbling desperately with his own blaster but without success. If only Chris could have used the helmet radio, he could have told the other fellow that help was at hand. At the risk of using too much power he released another small burst from his gun. He couldn't bear to let the other astronaut suffer mental agony a moment longer than was necessary.

When Tony found that his blaster wouldn't work and that nothing he could do would alter it, he had to fight down a feeling of panic. He forced himself to examine the gun as calmly as he could, but he could see nothing wrong from the outside. But he kept shaking it and pressing the trigger in the hope that a miracle might happen.

It did—but not in the way Tony expected. Suddenly something touched him. It was a hand on his shoulder, and as he spun round, he saw one of the most welcome sights it was possible to behold. A fellow astronaut, obviously aware of his plight, had come after him to help him back to Alpha. Relief flooded over Tony. His heart was pounding so much that, even if his radio had been usable, he would have been unable to speak.

Chris and Tony recognized each other, and Chris grinned encouragingly through his visor. In explanation Tony gestured toward his gun and Chris signaled to Tony to hold on to him while he used his own gun to propel them both back to the ship.

For a moment he thought he wouldn't have enough power in his blaster to kill their momentum and propel them both back to the ship. But the gun lasted out, and the two astronauts floated slowly toward Alpha. Even so, their direction wasn't quite accurate, and Chris had to expend the last ounce of his blaster's energy to set them on the right course. If they missed the ship even now, then space would claim two victims instead of one.

Fortunately, Tony was able to grab one of the handholds near the nose of the ship as they were floating past. Both he and Chris were pulled up with a jerk that nearly wrenched out Tony's arm, and they clung thankfully to the outer casing while they recovered themselves. Then,

Tony leading, they hauled themselves toward the airlock.

Tony entered Alpha first, and by the time Chris had followed him, he had had his helmet removed by the anxious crew, who had been watching through a porthole. There was no need for Tony to thank Chris. It was part of the job, and that was enough.

"Can we fix the frequencies?" Tony was saying when all the greetings were over. "We were wondering if, as a precaution, we ought to plan a whole sequence of frequency changes so that if Uranus chases us through the wavebands, we can keep one step ahead."

"We guessed that that was why you came across to us," Chris said. "Colin was already talking on the same lines. But if, as you say, Uranus chases us through the wavebands, it will become a very worrying situation. We can let each other know our plans, for we're close enough to make other trips if necessary. But it means we shall be cut off from Control, that is, unless they happen to hit upon our new frequencies."

"They'll do that, never fear," Tony declared. "Sir Billy will soon see if we're broadcasting on another wavelength. And if *he* doesn't think of it, Lord Benson will."

Then they drew up a list of frequencies which they would use, one after another, if necessary.

"How long will it take us to make the first change?" Norman Spier asked.

"I can manage it in a couple of hours," Colin announced. "How about you, Tony?"

"Give me time to get back to Beta, and I can rig our set up in about the same time."

"Say in three hours' time then," Chris said. "Now, what happened to that gun of yours?"

They examined the jet gun that had so nearly cost Tony his life. A small pin had fractured—a chance in a million, for every part had been carefully tested before the voyage began. The gun was put aside so that when they returned

34

to Earth, the makers could try to find the reason for the break.

"Now, are you quite sure you'll be all right to make the return?" Chris asked.

"Of course," Tony declared.

This time there was no mishap, and Tony made the journey back to Beta without incident. On this occasion he was too preoccupied to do any stargazing. He must concentrate on rigging the radio so that Uranus couldn't interfere—at least for a time.

"What happened?" demanded Serge as soon as his companions had helped Tony out of his suit.

"A wretched pin broke, and the gun jammed," Tony explained. "I thought I was in for rather a long journey."

"Thank goodness for radar," Serge breathed. "Who pulled you in?"

"Chris, of course," Tony repied gratefully. "Still—I managed to get over the list of frequencies, and he wants us to try them out in—" glancing at his watch—"two and a half hours' time."

While Tony made the necessary adjustments to the transmitter and the receiver, the rest of the crew carried out the routine inspection of the ship for meteor damage. All was well, and Tony completed his work before the time set for the broadcast. Now they could only wait. They hated being out of radio contact with each other. It was bad enough not to be able to communicate, but the knowledge that something from Uranus was responsible was really frightening.

"Ready?" Tony asked.

Serge nodded. After the few seconds it would take for the apparatus to warm up, they would know if their stratagem had succeeded. Then, if it had, the burning question would be—for how long will it stay that way?

"Hello, Beta, are you receiving me?"

The voice of Colin Johnson spluttered from the loudspeaker, and there was a relieved cheer from Beta's crew. Serge took the microphone and sent a message back. For about ten minutes the two ships exchanged greetings and information. Then, quite suddenly, the eerie howl of Uranus broke in, blotting out all communication.

Chris looked serious. He was almost convinced, now, that these broadcasts were not a natural phenomenon. It was hardly conceivable that the frequency of such a powerful radio signal could change of its own accord. Within a very short time of their own broadcast on the new wavelength, Uranus had detected it and changed its own frequency to match.

"Try the next one," Chris ordered, and Colin set to work to switch to the second frequency on the list. No doubt Tony would be at work doing the same. Uranus does the job more quickly than I can, thought Colin as he battled on. The second change was equally successful and the two ships talked together again.

"When Uranus comes in this time," Chris said, "instead of changing to the third wavelength, let's go back to our original one first. That will tell us if the planet is extending its range of transmissions, or just jumping about as we are."

"If Uranus leaves our original wavelength for a time we could, perhaps, get through to Control," Serge called back, and Chris agreed that this must be their prime objective. Some ten minutes after the new exchanges had begun, the voice of Uranus came flooding in, and the two crews had to switch off in disgust.

"Do as Chris says," Serge told Tony, and the mechanic set about changing their transmitter and receiver back to its original wavelength.

It was clear. As soon as the sets in the two ships had warmed up, they were able to talk together as before. Moreover, a voice from Control, somewhat distorted, was coming across space.

"—you receiving? Are you receiving us?" the anxious voice of the distant broadcaster was asking. "We are getting interference from the Uranus signals. Report your condition. Urgent."

Then the message was repeated several times, so Chris broadcast a concise report of what had happened and told Control about their switching of wavelengths. He gave a list of the frequencies they proposed to use between the ships so that Control could follow them, and explained that they had now found their original wavelength free, but expected interference at any moment. Had Control any instructions?

He had barely put the question when the hateful howls came through. Uranus had discovered their stratagem and was broadcasting strongly. Angrily both crews switched off and began the tedious task of once more adjusting their radios.

"I don't know how long we can keep this up," grumbled Colin as he fumbled with the apparatus in Alpha.

"We'll keep it up as long as necessary," Chris snapped, but his tone revealed how worried he was. In all his long experience in space, he had never encountered a problem like this. He'd never come across any sign of active intelligent life on any other planet in the solar system. True, he'd found traces of a long-dead civilization on Mars, now peopled with pure intelligences whose bodies had been evolved out of existence. And he'd come across living organisms in the atmosphere of Venus. Some he'd brought back to Earth in a successful bid to rid our planet of a deadly fungus that was threatening to destroy it.

But here was evidence of active intelligent life. And there was little doubt that it was malevolent. The persistent following of their frequency switches, the strange effect of the sounds transmitted seemed to indicate someone who was determined to ruin the expedition.

Why? Chris could only think that, whoever or whatever

it was on Uranus that was responsible, he or it had no intention of letting the ships get near.

But was this assumption really justified? As a scientist as well as an astronaut, Chris felt he couldn't be certain of the planet's hostility without much more evidence. It could be argued that someone, unaware of the harmful effects of his broadcasts, was trying desperately to communicate with Earth or with the crews of the two spaceships. To western ears some eastern languages sound very strange. Yet they are a means of exchanging thoughts between individuals. Might it not be that this strange, disturbing sound from Uranus was also an attempt to get over a message?

When contact was next established with Beta, Chris put his ideas to both crews. He didn't want them to assume that the presence on Uranus was necessarily evil or hostile toward them. To find out made it more essential than ever that their expedition should succeed. The matter couldn't be left in doubt.

Besides, the signals from Uranus were having an effect back on Earth. The situation must be clarified so that action could be taken. Sir Billy Gillanders had sounded a little worried in his last broadcast.

5

Sir billy certainly was worried. It was bad enough that the strange howls that came over the ether produced headaches. But it was worse that they should also be interfering with reception from the ships. Each time Control tried to pick up messages from either Alpha or Beta, the unearthly sounds came through and had to be promptly switched off. Billy tried taping the sounds and then playing them back. But the effect was the same. There was something in the wave pattern that had a devastating effect on human hearing.

It might eventually be possible to sort out the element of the wave pattern that was doing the damage. It might also be possible to eliminate it from the record. But all this would take time, and meanwhile anything might be happening to the two ships.

Quite suddenly, it was reported, the signals from Uranus had changed frequency. It was as if whoever was responsible for their transmission had suddenly decided to try a different wavelength. Now that the band usually used for communication with the ships was relatively free, Control made redoubled efforts to make contact. Every available receiver was tuned in to the ships' wavelength, and the powerful transmitter at the Cape sent a constant beam of messages in the direction of the ships.

Sir Billy seriously contemplated recalling the expedition if he could get his order through. Yet all had seemed well aboard Alpha and Beta when they last reported. Now that the planet was so close—a mere two weeks' journey away—he was reluctant to waste all the effort that had been put into mounting the exercise. More must be discovered about the signals. Otherwise radio communication on Earth might become impossible.

It was just after the director had decided to allow the expedition to proceed that the receivers at Control picked up Chris's message. It explained all that had happened and repeated the list of frequencies they proposed to try. This would at least, it seemed, decoy the broadcasts from Control's wavelength and enable them to speak with Earth every so often. Had Control any instructions?

Control had no special instructions to send back. Sir Billy would arrange for the widest possible waveband to be used both for reception and broadcasts. Meanwhile, it would be as well for both crews to make their final spell in the fridge last until ETA –24. That is—estimated time of arrival, minus twenty-four hours. The ships were on course, and there was little the crews could do until they made the final approach to their target.

Then Chris would have the vital decision to make—at what distance should the ships go into orbit? Should they go in at a fairly safe distance from the planet, or should he take his two ships as close as possible to try to discover the exact source of the voice? Meanwhile, all the resources at the disposal of UNEXA could concentrate on trying to analyze the recordings of the signals. Perhaps by the time the crews were defrosted, Sir Billy would have some useful suggestions to make.

One thing the director decided almost at once. He would invite his old friend and former chief to be at his side during the critical period. Lord Benson, he knew, would need no second asking once he was sure that Billy really wanted and needed him.

That decided, the director arranged for a message of encouragement to be broadcast simultaneously on each of the wavelengths Chris had indicated. This would make sure that, no matter which of the frequencies they were using at the time, the crews would get their instruction to enter the fridge for the last time before reaching Uranus. Then Sir Billy packed his bags and flew to England.

Lord Benson was, of course, delighted to receive a visit from his old friend, particularly when it brought an invitation to return with him to the Cape. The former director still found his retirement more than a little irksome, all the more since he knew that the Uranus expedition would soon be reaching a critical stage.

Since his last visit to Cape Kennedy, Lord Benson had been devoting much thought to the significance of the radio signals. Like Chris, he'd decided not to regard them as hostile until there was more definite proof. The strange effect the sounds had on human listeners might well be accidental. Was there any real evidence that the signals came from intelligent beings?

Sir Billy had not only let the former director have a tape recording of some of the signals, he'd also supplied him with many yards of the paper strip showing the trace of the strange sounds. Lord Benson had experimented with the tapes and had found that the volume of the signals made little difference to their effect. It was true that when the volume was so low as to be inaudible, the effect was somewhat reduced. But it was still noticeable.

Then he fixed a very long remote-control switch to his own tape recorder. He placed the instrument on a table in his large garden and moved away. At a certain distance he would switch on the tape of the voice and note its effect. Even at sixty yards he found that the signals affected his head. But this time he'd come to the end of his remote-control cable, and he wondered if it was any use continuing his experiment. However, he decided to carry on, and drove to the local electricians for another drum of cable.

He now found he had to go into the lane outside his garden in order to get farther away from his tape recorder, so he decided to extend the new cable to its limit at once. When he switched on, he was surprised to note that the voice no longer affected him, even though he increased the volume so that he could hear the tape at this distance of 150 yards.

Lord Benson became more and more fascinated with the problem and spent the next two days in experimenting. As a result, he discovered that the harmful effect of the voice extended to a distance of 110 yards from the source of the sound—the tape recorder—and that the volume made little difference. A telephone call to Jodrell Bank ensured the delivery of a tape of the signals recorded by the giant dish direct from the planet. The result was the same.

"So it's not the sound itself," he mused. "If it were, then the effect would be apparent wherever it was audible."

There must be something concealed within, and masked by, the sound wave that was causing such devastating results. Lord Benson had a close look at the paper records of the voice of Uranus.

Careful scrutiny revealed that, apart from the usual waverings of the recording pen, there was an almost invisible quiver on portions of the track. He looked at these anxiously, for he'd never seen anything like them before. Could this be a clue to what he was seeking? The only way to find out was to try to re-create a similar wave pattern and to see if these artificial vibrations had the same effect.

Lord Benson was well satisfied with his efforts, and he told Sir Billy about his theory. Of course he had no laboratory, and would be unable to carry his investigations further without the help of experts. Billy was intrigued with what his old friend had said and promised to give him everything he needed.

Benson was now torn between the desire to continue his research and the wish to rush to the Cape for the planetary approach. It was important to try to unravel the mystery of the Uranus signals, but he wanted, more than anything else, to share in the astronauts' moments of triumph or disaster. Eventually he reached a compromise with himself. He would work for a further week on the problem of the radio transmissions, and then fly to Florida in time for the crews' last awakening before they went into orbit around Uranus.

Sir Billy, satisfied that he'd left his friend usefully occupied, flew back to Cape Kennedy. The two ships were dead on course and were now decelerating. Signals from the planet were blotting out the usual communication wavelength more strongly than ever, though fortunately the telemetry wavelengths seemed reasonably clear. Control was thus able to keep track of the two ships while their crews were frozen and was also able to dispatch certain commands to pieces of automatic apparatus.

"It seems that the interference comes on the voice channels only," Dr. Rosenberg, one of Sir Billy's deputies, told his chief as they discussed the flight together. Billy thought this piece of information was sufficiently significant to warrant a phone call to Lord Benson, and in reply was told that the former director had now definitely identified the cause of the signals' audible effect. He'd managed to reproduce the voice of Uranus without the minute superimposed quivers and the sound had had no effect on anyone who had listened to it.

"Interesting," Billy told him over the long-distance phone. "Now can you reproduce the quivers alone?"

"That's what I'm working on," Benson replied. "I'll let you know if I succeed."

43

Sir Billy turned his attention back to the expedition. There were still a few days to run before the crews were defrosted, and the director spent the time in reviewing a number of contingency plans that Control had proposed to meet any unexpected happening.

This was the period when the scientists and technicians on duty in the long main hall of Control were beginning to get very worked up. After long weeks of routine tracking of the ships they would soon be faced with a period of intense activity. Every man and woman knew that he or she would have a vital part to play in deciding whether the expedition would be a success or a disaster. The lives of the eight brave young men—so many millions of miles away—might depend on the alertness of any one of them.

The hundreds of instruments that were recording conditions on board the two ships must be watched constantly. If any member of the Control staff allowed his or her attention to wander, some vital piece of information that called for instant action might be missed. Sir Billy and his deputies had the hardest job. With them lay the ultimate responsibility for decisions, but they must appear calm and confident at all times.

Two days before the crews were due to be awakened, Lord Benson came to the Cape. He'd been unable, so far, to duplicate the tiny quivers from Uranus, and he couldn't bear to postpone his visit any longer. Sir Billy gave him the free run of Control, and he spent some hours informing himself about the present state of the expedition. When he'd finished, Sir Billy invited him to sit in at a conference he'd called to discuss the radio signals.

There were about a dozen scientists gathered in the director's office, and Lord Benson knew all but two of them.

"This is Dr. Tongue and this is Mr. Scott," Sir Billy said. Benson shook hands with both.

"Let's summarize what we know," Sir Billy began. "The signals were first detected about a year ago, and since then there has been a steady increase in their strength. Their source has been definitely located on or near Uranus. The signals, in the audible range, consist of a whistling note that rises and falls, followed by a short period of silence. One complete cycle lasts ninety-four seconds and is extremely constant.

"It soon became evident that the transmissions were having a strange effect on human listeners. Considerable distress is caused to anyone who hears these signals for more than a fraction of a second. You all know what I mean, and it seems that we cannot listen in to the Uranus signals unaided. However, thanks to some valuable work by our colleague, Lord Benson, the element in the transmissions which is causing the distress has been identified. George, will you tell us what you found?"

Lord Benson was more grateful than he could say at being thus involved once more in research with former colleagues. Even though his contribution might be small and unimportant, at least it was a contribution.

"When I examined the trace on the paper record," he said, "I noticed an almost imperceptible quiver concealed within the main track. With the aid of some tapes that the director was good enough to lend me, I made a few experiments. I found, first of all, that the volume of the signals is not an important factor in causing the distress. What counts is the distance from the source of the sound. Thus, when the volume was reduced until the signals were inaudible, distress was still caused to an observer standing within a hundred and ten yards. Beyond that distance, even though the volume was increased, no harmful effects were observed.

"Furthermore, I have had a recording made of the Uranus signals without the quivers. They are quite harmless. Work is now proceeding to see if we can produce the quivers without the signals."

"Thank you, George," Sir Billy resumed. "Now, one of

the most disturbing features of these radio signals is the way they switch frequencies. As you know, the crews were unable to communicate either with each other or with us until they had switched to another wavelength. Then, within a very short time, the Uranus signals were being transmitted on the new wavelength. This has been repeated several times, and it is difficult to keep a jump ahead of the Uranus broadcasts."

"So you think there is a 'broadcaster'?" Dr. Tongue asked.

"I can't think of any natural phenomenon that would produce such results. Can you?" Billy replied.

No one could. Although several of the people present were radio experts or top astronauts, no one had ever experienced anything like the peculiar behavior of the Uranus signals.

"Another strange thing," Billy went on, "is that these transmissions only come through on our voice wavelengths. The telemetry frequencies have, fortunately, been left alone. Any suggestions?"

"If these are signals from an intelligence, then it seems that it is trying to speak to us," Dr. Rosenberg suggested.

It was a disturbing thought. Science-fiction stories had often described the first encounter between humans and beings from another world. But these had been just stories which one could read in the comfort of an armchair. Here, in these signals from Uranus, was a sign that an encounter might be imminent.

Man, in his isolation, had come to regard himself as the highest form of life in the universe. All his customs and beliefs were built on that assumption. Though scientists had, for years, been preaching that life elsewhere was possible, the man in the street had never really accepted the idea. Clinging to the belief in his uniqueness, he had listened to the scientists with tolerant good humor. How could there be a higher form of life? he asked himself proudly as he looked around at his pubs and bingo halls, his motor cars and frozen foods, his high rises and slums.

Sir Billy recaptured the attention of his audience by suggesting that they should all keep an open mind about the signals. They required still more proof before deciding if they were natural or artificial. And if they were artificial, still more information would be needed before they could know whether the aliens were friendly or hostile.

Chris and his crews would soon find the answer.

6

ABOUT THIRTY HOURS before it was time to go into orbit, the crews of the two ships began to defrost for the last time. That is—the last time until after their mission had been successfully completed.

This time it was Tony, in Beta, who first sat up on his couch. Without stopping to look at his companions, he swung from his resting place, made for the hatch into the cabin, and hurried over to the observation window. And what a sight met his eyes!

Uranus filled almost his whole field of view. It was as if the planet had suddenly leaped near to the spaceship, for the last time Tony had looked—was it just a few minutes ago?—it had seemed no larger than a basketball. Now it was peering through the spaceship's window with a pale-green light.

He gazed at it with wonder. Though most of the planet seemed to be colored a pale, pearly green, there were patches of a darker shade, and even some of blue. Then there were two almost white areas that reminded Tony of the Martian ice caps. It all looked indescribably beautiful.

"Beautiful it is indeed!" said the voice of Mervyn. The Welshman had joined his friend at the window and was now looking through at the amazing sight beyond. His face was ecstatic, and Tony almost expected him to burst into song.

"Yes, but don't forget that this is where the radio signals are coming from," he reminded him.

The mercurial Mervyn was silent. What would happen when they switched on their radios? Would the voice of Uranus blare out more loudly than ever? What was lurking down beneath those pearly clouds? Was there some intelligent creature, good or evil, awaiting them below?

Within a few minutes the rest of Beta's crew were gazing with wonder at the vast, mysterious world outside.

"Come on," said Serge at last, "we have work to do."

Robert Campbell was detailed to the external inspection of the ship, and while Serge and Mervyn began a close scrutiny of the interior, Tony prepared to call up Alpha on the radio. He knew exactly to which wavelength to switch if Uranus should be broadcasting.

Meanwhile, Robert stood in the airlock ready to open the outer door. Strangely enough, he was hesitating. Now that they were all so near to the giant planet, the home of the strange broadcaster, what would the next few hours reveal? He knew he was about to come face to face with something no man had met before. He was about to gaze directly at the vast, luminous sphere that might be the home of an entirely different form of life.

Then his training asserted itself. He pressed the switch that would cause the outer door to swing open—and waited for the result.

If Uranus had seemed impressive when viewed through the cabin window, it was truly astounding when seen through empty space. The vast ball seemed to have even more shades of color. And as he watched, Robert could detect a slow change.

Patches of blue gradually faded, and others appeared in different places. The basic green color of the major part of the planet fluctuated in intensity. At some moments it would appear a delicate, pearly green, and at others it would look a much harsher shade. Instead of being placid, the cloud layer of Uranus was in a state of turmoil, and Robert wondered what tremendous forces were at work that could bring about changes on so large a scale. But he must get on with his task.

It was with some apprehension that Tony switched on the radio. The first job was to report to Chris in Alpha and the second to contact Control. Would the voice of Uranus let him? For a few moments the wavelength was clear, but before he could wire their sister ship, the dreaded sounds came flooding in.

Tony was a little worried. The crew of Alpha must still be under hypothermia, and when they revived, they would immediately switch on to the wavelength now invaded. He must divert the voice to another frequency so that, for a brief time, the original radio channel would be clear. He set about his task swiftly and with skill. Soon he was calling out to their sister ship but, of course, without response. Then, within the usual ten minutes, the voice had found the frequency and was flooding it.

"Anyway, that's cleared it away from the usual wavelength," Tony consoled himself.

But he was wrong! When he tried to call Alpha, the voice was waiting. It was broadcasting on both wavelengths!

Tony told Serge of his discovery, and the Russian looked grave.

"It seems that the creature has discovered our plan," he said. "If this goes on, it can blot out all our channels."

It meant that all communication, not only with Alpha but with Control, would eventually be impossible. While this wouldn't prevent the expedition from proceeding, it would make its continuance very risky. Instant contact between Alpha and Beta had been a very important part of the flight plan.

The crew of Alpha were now reviving, and it wasn't long before Chris, too, had discovered what the voice had done. The problem was, on what wavelength would it be possible to contact Beta? True, the ships were both working to the agreed list, but at what point would they meet? Colin Johnson, at the radio, would be a very busy man.

Eventually contact was made. Chris and Serge exchanged a further list of frequencies that they would try, but this couldn't go on forever. They hadn't the resources or the range of equipment to dodge the voice for long. It was a worrying situation. However, both crews were immensely cheered to hear Control. Broadcast on a wide range of frequencies, Control was able to tell them what had been discovered about the Uranus broadcasts.

It was Tony who seized on the most interesting piece of information. Uranus was only broadcasting on the voice channels. The telemetry frequencies seemed to have been left alone. Could it be that whoever was responsible thought that humans communicated by voice alone? Didn't the voice know what an immense amount of information was constantly conveyed to the hundreds of instruments at the Cape over the telemetry channels?

Then why not try speaking to each other without using the human voice? Would the broadcaster on Uranus recognize Morse as a means of speaking to each other? It was worth trying.

Tony told Serge of his idea and the Russian agreed immediately. But would such a simple device delude the Uranian intelligence? If the broadcaster was able to detect and defeat their scheme of changing frequencies, wouldn't he also be able to recognize communication even if it was by Morse code? There was only one thing to do. Try it!

Both spaceships were equipped with the latest and most sophisticated instruments possible, but neither had the very simple instrument that Tony needed, a Morse tapper. He could make what he wanted, but Alpha would have to have it, too. So when the two ships managed their next brief conversation, Tony explained his plan to Chris.

Colin set about his task just as Tony was doing in the

other ship. Both astronauts regarded it as a test of their ingenuity to be able to make the Morse equipment. As Colin worked and as the instruments began to take shape, Chris couldn't help a few rueful reflections.

Here, in this age of advanced forms of communication both in radio and television, they were being forced to use one of the most primitive. Chris remembered from his history books how the Morse telegraph had been invented and what a wonderful thing it was thought to be. It had meant that messages could be exchanged over long distances through the telegraph wires. He could picture the old operators tapping out their messages to someone a hundred miles away, and then the buzzer would chatter in reply. These telegraphists had become very efficient and had been able to transmit and read messages at quite a high speed.

Chris himself didn't know the Morse code too well, but Tony and Colin did. He must polish it up without delay, he told himself. As leader of the expedition he must understand the signals that were being flashed between the two ships and Control. For if this ruse worked, Control too would have to produce an old-fashioned Morse key. He could well imagine how this would look among all the wonderful gadgets with which that long room was littered. Anyhow—Control would be luckier than his crews. Tony and Colin were having to make their equipment from all sorts of bits and pieces. Sir Billy would be able to raid the nearest science museum to get what he wanted.

Meanwhile, Robert had returned to Beta and Norman to Alpha after their EVA. Both were able to give reassuring reports on the external condition of the ships, and no damage had been found in either of the interiors. So all was set for a near approach to the lovely, yet menacing, planet.

The deadline for testing out the Morse equipment was

fast approaching. It had been arranged that at a given moment, and on an agreed wavelength, the two ships should try to communicate. Tony had completed his task and was impatient to use the result. In Alpha, Colin Johnson was ready and waiting, too. At a nod from Chris he began tapping out his message. It wasn't a very long one, for Colin wasn't as adept as Tony, so the messages had to be brief.

"VELOCITY SIXTH THOUSAND, DISTANCE NINE HUNDRED THOUSAND. WILL CLOSE TO HALF MILL. FOR ORBIT DECISION," it said.

There was a brief pause, and the crew of Alpha began to wonder if their message had got across. Then their loudspeaker began to sound out the reply.

"RECEIVED YOU CLEARLY. HOW FAR DOWN SHALL WE GO? SHALL WE SHOOT SATS?"

"He'll have to go a bit slower," Colin groaned as he struggled to write down Tony's fluent transmission. "Have I got it right, Chris?"

"It seems all right," Chris assured his friend. "Tony is asking if they're to take observations on the satellites. Just send back 'YES, SHOOT.'"

Colin did as Chris asked, and then added his own plea for Tony to go a little more slowly.

Chris became very thoughtful. Uranus had, he knew, a family of five satellites, and he smiled to himself as he recalled their names. Someone fancifully christened four of them after well-known Shakespearian characters: Oberon, Titania, Ariel, and Miranda. The fifth satellite is called Umbriel. Before long the ships would be as close as Oberon, which perpetually circles Uranus at a distance of three hundred and sixty-four thousand miles.

What would it be like on Oberon? The satellite is about two thirds the size of our Moon, and its gravity would, therefore, be weak—far too weak to retain any atmosphere. And it would be incredibly cold, of course. The surface would probably be rocky and pitted with meteor craters—an inhospitable place indeed.

But inhospitable to whom? Man could exist on Oberon with the utmost difficulty, but did that necessarily mean that another life form couldn't live there? It hadn't been established from where precisely on Uranus the radio signals were coming. Could their source possibly be on one of the satellites?

On reflection Chris didn't think so, for then the radio signals would disappear when the satellite was on the far side of the planet, just as it was impossible to speak directly with Earth from the lunar base on the far side of the Moon. The body of the planet would mask any signals sent out, and there seemed to have been no interruption in their reception. Stations on Earth had been receiving the voice for a year and a half.

But wait a minute! There could be an explanation of that. As Chris recalled, one of the most peculiar things about Uranus is that, unlike any other planet, its axis is almost in line with its orbit. That means, roughly, that in its movement round the Sun, the planet seems to be lying on its side. At certain periods one of the poles would be toward the Earth, and at others the equator would be nearest. These periods are approximately twenty-one years long. Now when one of the poles is facing the Earth, satellites—which move round the equator—would be in sight of Earth for twenty-one years without once disappearing. So it was possible for the radio signals to be coming from one of the satellites! For in their pre-flight briefing, Chris and the others had been told that they were in the middle of a period when the Uranian north pole was facing the Earth.

Decidedly, the satellites couldn't be ruled out as possible sites for the transmitter. From their position now it should be possible to get a fix on the source. Tony would have to rig up something that could tune into the signals without converting them into sound. Possibly he could adapt one of the radio scanners for the job so that the signals became visual instead of audible.

Accordingly, Chris wrote down a fairly lengthy message for Colin to tap across to Beta. Tony acknowledged and promised to set to work at once. If they could pinpoint the spot where the transmitter was, it would be an important step toward the accomplishment of the mission.

As Tony worked away, he congratulated himself on the success of his ruse. The two ships had been "talking" to each other for nearly two hours, and there was no sign of interference from Uranus. Control, too, must soon be getting their Morse signals and would no doubt reply in the same manner. It would be a relief to reestablish this direct contact with Sir Billy and his team, even though the process would be a tedious one.

For the next few hours the crews of both ships performed their routine duties, except for Tony and Colin. The former was immersed in the construction of an instrument to locate the voice, and the latter was battling manfully to transmit by Morse to Control as much information as possible.

"My arm will drop off any minute now," Colin moaned as he tapped away with the Morse key.

It was an exciting moment for both crews when messages began to come in from Control, though there was no time for the usual flow of jokes.

Sir Billy and Lord Benson both sent messages of encouragement to the eight astronauts, but this was the only departure from the terse exchange of information. The gist of it was that the two ships were now just under seven hundred thousand miles from the planet and still decelerating. The steady thrust of the atomic motors had been doing their work while the two crews were frozen. In a few hours Chris might decide to switch to the chemical engines for a more rapid slowdown.

Control had quickly recognized the switch to Morse, but was continuing to monitor the Uranian signals on the former channels. The voice was coming through on each of these more strongly than ever, and work was still continuing in an effort to analyze the signals. Meanwhile, the astronauts must, if possible, avoid audible contact with their objective.

"I must be getting tired," Colin Johnson suddenly declared, pushing his pencil and paper away from him. He'd been coping valiantly with the incoming signals from both Control and Beta. He'd scribbled down the messages as he'd read them from the speaker while Chris had ripped a sheet at a time from Colin's notepad. Now Chris looked at his colleague with concern.

"What's the matter?" he asked. "Feel queer?"

"I—I don't seem able to concentrate," Colin muttered. "I'm not reading the signals correctly."

Chris glanced down at the top sheet of the note pad. It was covered with a meaningless jumble of letters which he couldn't make sense of. Colin had certainly cracked up if this was his reading of the incoming signals.

"Have a rest for a spell," Chris told him. "I'll try to take over."

Though he knew his Morse wasn't even as good as Colin's, Chris could read the signals, and if this was the gibberish that Colin was making of his task, then he had no option but to relieve him for a time. Chris sat in Colin's place and took over the pencil and notepad. Then he concentrated on the speaker at his side. But in less than thirty seconds he, too, had given up the task.

"This is rubbish," he exclaimed, glancing down at what he'd written on the pad.

There was the same meaningless jumble of letters that Colin had been writing. What had happened? Had someone at Control or in Beta gone crazy? Or had their equipment developed a fault? During a pause in the incoming signals he tapped a message across to their sister ship, demanding to know if they were sending these strange signals. And at once the reply came back that they were not and were equally puzzled.

Then something must have happened at Control, but it would be some hours before he could check. It was useless to record the stuff that was coming in. He would have to wait for a pause so that he could transmit his request for an explanation to Control. But surely, with the facilities at his disposal, Sir Billy would have taken steps to replace a faulty instrument or a crazy operator before now. Chris felt in his bones that there must be another explanation.

It couldn't be, could it, that these strange messages were not coming from Earth at all? Surely it wasn't Uranus again?

Chris had a dreadful feeling that it was.

7

THE SOUNDS that filled the cabin from the radio were just the same as the signals from Beta. Anyone who didn't know Morse wouldn't detect any difference. It was only when the signals were transcribed that their strangeness became apparent.

"OONYPXJKV TRAL WVJ," Chris had written down. The other three astronauts bent over the notepad, but no one could make sense of the jumble of letters. Quietly, Chris explained his theory. The broadcaster on Uranus—or one of its satellites—had, after some delay, detected their new means of communication and was again intruding.

"What do we do now?" Morrey asked.

"I know," Norman said brightly, "let's talk back to that chap in his own language."

Chris smiled in spite of himself.

"I doubt whether this is a language," he said, looking down at the paper. "It's just our interpretation of what the signals would be if they were Morse. Actually, it's probably just a series of long and short whistles that we transcribed as if they were our own signals."

"At least I'm glad to know it isn't me who's crazy," Colin said more cheerfully. "What do you want me to do, Chris?"

"Well, just to satisfy Norman, repeat these letters back to the sender," the leader replied.

Colin took over the tapper and spelled out the Uranian's "message."

"OONYPXJKV TRAL WVJ."

"Hope he understands it better than we do," Morrey said drily. "What will he say next?"

The answer came in a few seconds, for the Uranian repeated his original message twice. Colin replied similarly.

Beta had been listening in to these exchanges.

"What's happening?" Tony tapped out.

"We're trying to talk to Uranus," Colin spelled back. "We've let him know we've picked up his signals simply by repeating them to him."

Even now the proof that there was an intelligent creature on Uranus was not conclusive. There might be some natural explanation for the signals. Tony remembered one occasion back on Earth when he thought someone was signaling in Morse. It was a dark night, and there was a high wind. In the distance he saw a series of flashes of light that he began to read off. All he got was a meaningless jumble of letters like that from Uranus.

Was it a code? Was it a foreign language? Almost convinced he was on the track of a spy, Tony had made his way cautiously to where the signals were coming from. And there he'd found that they were caused by two overhead wires being blown together by the wind.

"Can I try him with numbers?" Tony tapped across to Chris.

"Go ahead," the message came back.

So Tony tapped out a series of signals. One signal. Pause. Two signals. Pause. Three signals. Pause. Four signals.

Then everyone waited breathlessly for a reply. It soon came. One signal. Pause. Two signals. Pause. Three signals. Pause. Four signals. Pause. Five signals!

"Got that, Chris?" Tony called over the radio. In his excitement he'd forgotten about the uncomfortable sounds from the planet that had made their radios useless.

"Yes, I got that," Chris's voice came clearly. "It looks as if he's cleared from this wavelength."

It was true. Tony and Colin between them tested all the frequencies that had been blocked by the strange broadcaster. They were all clear.

"Maybe he'll leave them clear now he's established a channel of communication," Chris said thoughtfully.

Tony continued his efforts with the Uranian. After reciprocating signals up to about twenty, he switched to another series of numbers; 3, 6, 9, he sent out. The Uranian promptly replied with 12, 15, 18, and 21. Then Tony broadcast 3, 9, 27, to which he got a quick answer, 81.

"This chap's pretty smart," he observed to Chris over the radio.

"There's no doubt about it," Chris said to the rest of the crew, "we've established beyond doubt that there is an intelligence behind those signals."

It was a tremendous moment. For the first time in human history they had proof of the existence of other creatures. The possibility had been dreamed about and speculated upon for centuries. A whole literature had sprung up about the imaginary inhabitants of other worlds. But that had been pure fiction—or perhaps wishful thinking. There had never before been any definite evidence of the existence of such beings.

Now all that was over. It was no longer a matter of speculation, of perhaps hope or fear. It was a fact. Something or someone did exist. And that someone not only had highly developed radio, but also wished to get into touch with the Earthmen. The signals that had started to come across space, uncomfortable though they were, had been the Uranian's attempt to contact humans. Now that Morse signals had been exchanged, the Uranian was concentrating on them and seemed to have abandoned his earlier broadcasts.

Taking advantage of the freedom of the voice channels, Chris spoke long and earnestly to Control. He told them of their astounding discovery and how the Uranian had replied to their sequences of numbers. Would Control advise on further exchanges?

Chris was now convinced that the Uranians meant them no harm. It was just bad luck that their first broadcasts had upset humans so much. Now that the switch had been made to Morse signals, the Uranian seemed anxious to cooperate. His prompt reply to the astronaut's broadcasts had proved this. It had also proved that he knew the science of numbers.

How could they extend the contact? How does one exchange ideas with a creature whose language one cannot speak, who perhaps has no language as we know it? On Earth it is possible to learn languages, even without the help of teachers and textbooks. For here we have visual means of explaining what sounds mean. The tenuous contact with the Uranian was by radio signals only. It would seem to be an impossible task to converse.

In the excitement aroused in the two ships by this discovery, further work had been overlooked. Now Serge returned to his task of observing the moons of Uranus, while Tony put the finishing touches to his direction finder. Because Uranus was now transmitting harmless Morse buzzes, a simple piece of apparatus would reveal the direction the signals were coming from. It would no longer be necessary to convert one of the radar scanners to do the job.

Serge had now pinpointed the five moons of Uranus. Oberon, Titania and Ariel were easily located, for they were all of a similar size—about two thirds that of our Moon. The others were more difficult, for Umbriel has a diameter of only eight hundred miles, while Miranda is very tiny, having one of a mere two hundred miles. Yet there they all were, scattered round their planet and circling it at different speeds.

Though Uranus is large, its family of satellites scurry round it very quickly. The outer moon, Oberon, takes only half as long to go round Uranus as our Moon takes to go round Earth, even though Uranus is larger than Earth. Tiny little Miranda, the satellite nearest the planet, goes once round Uranus every thirty hours! Ariel, almost the twin to Oberon, wheels round his master in two and a half days!

"It's coming from Ariel," Tony suddenly announced.

The rest of the crew all turned toward him. Surely enough, the signals were coming most strongly from the direction of Ariel.

So the broadcaster wasn't on the surface of Uranus itself! He wasn't below those whirling clouds of methane and ammonia that were so poisonous to man. Instead he was riding along on the cloudless Ariel, that swift little copy of our own Moon.

Somehow the knowledge that the Uranian—perhaps he should no longer be called that—was in an environment with which the astronauts were familiar made him much more credible. Each of the crewmen had spent long periods on our Moon, and were quite used to the rigors of life on its surface. Ariel was somewhat smaller, even colder, completely airless, and, presumably, had the same barren and pitted surface.

Chris at once radioed the information to Control. At least they now had something to show for their expedition. Then another thought struck him. The two ships were now less than four hundred thousand miles from the surface of Uranus, close enough to detect other radio broadcasts if they existed.

The fact that the signals were coming from one place only in the Uranian system—Ariel—was intriguing. If Uranus or any of its moons had produced an intelligent form of life, surely there would be signals coming from many points. It seemed, on the face of it, that there was only one lone broadcaster on all that huge planet and its five satellites. And yet the power of the signals was remarkable. On Earth they were causing trouble, and their increasing strength had been a source of comment.

Another question presented itself to Chris. Why was it that the signals from Ariel had been received only during the last year? Any race that had developed sufficiently to be able to broadcast must have been in existence for a long time. Signals from Ariel could have been received quite clearly forty-two years before, when all the moons of Uranus were previously in continuous radio "sight" of Earth. Or the signals could have come intermittently at any time during the period when Ariel's orbit was taking it behind its primary planet.

The more Chris thought about the problem, the more interesting it became. There was definitely an intelligent —a highly intelligent—creature making the broadcasts. Once contact had been established by Morse, the harmful signals had ceased, showing that the broadcaster meant no ill, but was only concerned with communicating. There must be only one transmitting station, and it was of fairly recent origin. All this led Chris to such a startling theory that he dared not even mention it to his friends.

Both Alpha and Beta transmitted to Ariel. Each ship spelled out its own name in Morse, and the astronauts judged that Ariel had soon learned that two ships were approaching. He buzzed out each name in turn, followed by an unintelligible message. However, in each message there were the letters VARI.

"I wonder if that's his call sign. Or perhaps his name," Tony mused.

After that each of the ships began its message with Vari's name and ended with its own. It seemed that this was the thing to do, for Vari did the same thing in reverse.

"We're increasing our field of communication," Chris said excitedly to Morrey. "If only we could learn Vari's language!"

By this time messages came pouring in from Control. Sir Billy was on the radio frequently, and it seemed that he, too, appreciated the significance of the radio signals.

"We're picking up his Morse, but we can't make anything of it yet," the director's voice said. "However, we're getting our top philologists on it."

"Philologists? What are those?" Tony asked.

"Specialists in language," Serge told him. "They're people who make a special study of the structure of language. If anyone can understand what Vari is saying, they can."

"Yes, but they're only experts in earthly languages," Mervyn Williams pointed out. "Perhaps they will not be able to understand this one."

"If they can understand your heathen tongue, then they will make sense of this one for sure," spluttered Robert Campbell.

Before an argument could develop between the Welshman and the Ulsterman, Chris's voice came booming across space.

"We're changing course to go into orbit," he announced. Then followed instructions about the firing of lateral rockets to deflect the two ships. If they were successful, Alpha and Beta would be circling Uranus at about the same distance that the Moon is from Earth. That would give the astronauts a breathing space to plan the next move. Control was informed and was requested to furnish Chris with accurate details of the orbits of the two ships as soon as these had been worked out by the giant computer at the Cape.

The transfer into orbit seemed to have been accomplished successfully, though it would be some hours before Chris would get the full data from Control. Meanwhile, Sir Billy reported something else of interest.

"We're not getting any response to any of the signals we send out," he told the astronauts. "It seems he doesn't want to talk to us. He's only interested in you."

It was certainly strange, Vari, it seemed, had first directed his signals to Earth. But now two Earth ships had been sent to seek him, he was concentrating on making contact only with the crews.

"What are we going to do now?" Tony radioed his question across to Chris.

"We're going to await instructions from the Cape," the answer came back. "Meanwhile, let everyone get some rest and food."

8

"WE'RE CERTAINLY getting somewhere now," the director said to Lord Benson. "What do you make of it, Benny?"

Benson was as excited as his friend.

"I agree. This is the first definite contact we've ever had with someone from another system. Whoever is broadcasting to the ships must come from outside our solar system. To me it seems that a newcomer has landed on Ariel. Certainly a new situation must have developed."

"It's a frightening thought," Billy said slowly. "One can hardly imagine what a creature from another solar system must be like. It could well be extremely hostile."

"Nonsense," Lord Benson declared. "If the creature has developed an intelligence capable of sending and receiving radio signals, and capable of switching frequencies as rapidly as our friend has done, there is reason to believe that we shall have nothing to fear. A highly developed creature with those capabilities would be curious about us but not, I'm certain, hostile."

"You may be right, Benny," the director said doubtfully. "In any case, Chris and the others may soon find out."

Which was exactly what Chris intended to do. He'd been thinking very much along the same lines as Lord Benson, and having exchanged signals with Vari, he was even more convinced that the stranger wasn't dangerous. However, it was his duty to make direct contact and to pass all the information he could back to Control. If, indeed, Vari was a threat to the human race, then Chris would have to get a warning back somehow.

Was Vari on Ariel by design or accident? That was the question that interested Chris most. He was almost inclined to believe that Vari was a space wanderer and had somehow got "shipwrecked" on the Uranian moon. Perhaps his signals had been calls for help, even though, at first, they had been rather alarming.

On the other hand, this intruder from outer space might have chosen Ariel as a base from which to explore the solar system. With the radio equipment he appeared to have, he would be well aware that there was an intelligent race on the planet Earth. Radio signals from Earth had been transmitted for almost a century, and—traveling at the speed of light—they would have covered only a small fraction of the Universe. Nevertheless, our broadcasts would now have reached many solar systems—assuming that there were instruments sufficiently sensitive to receive them. Vari could well come from one of these solar systems that had picked up Earth signals, and his mission was obviously to find out more.

So it was that Chris decided to reveal his thoughts to his two crews. By radio link he spoke to the quartet in Beta as well as his companions in his own ship. There was quite a lively discussion afterward, but in the end all agreed that their leader could well be right.

"What are we going to do now?" Tony asked over the radio.

"The obvious thing to do is to land on Ariel and to find Vari," Chris replied promptly. "So what I've decided to do is to take Alpha in while Beta gets into orbit round the satellite. We can't both go in at the same time in case—well, just in case there is trouble."

"Don't you think you had better remain in orbit and let us take Beta in?" Tony asked hopefully.

"Not a chance," Chris called back. "It's my job to see what this Vari chap is like."

Tony knew that it was no use arguing with his leader, though he would dearly have loved to be one of the first humans to meet an alien from another world. The thought that the alien might be dangerous had crossed Tony's mind, but having exchanged messages with Vari, having almost played a game of numbers with him, he really didn't think that he would do them harm.

"Lock on to Ariel," Chris ordered Morrey, who was navigating at the time. Morrey gave the necessary instructions to the rest of the crew, while Chris sent a long message back to Control telling them of his theories and just what he proposed to do. If anything went wrong, it would be as well for Sir Billy to know what was happening.

Morrey had spotted the pinpoint of light that was their immediate objective. It was difficult to detect Ariel against the glare of Uranus, but he was confident he was right. Norman Spier, his bald head glistening as he bent over his task, fed data into the ship's small computer. Very soon it began to type out the answer. Chris looked at the paper carefully. It told him exactly what to do to overtake Ariel and to land on its surface.

"Serge, we're going in," Chris called over the radio to Beta. "Follow us and then get ready to go into orbit. Keep chatting to Vari meanwhile to keep him happy."

A few bursts of the lateral thrusters slightly altered Alpha's course. In a few hours the ship would overtake the swift little moon. Then Chris would have to select a spot on which to land his craft. He would want to get as near as possible to where Vari was broadcasting. And that would be the critical moment of the whole expedition.

While the two ships were streaking after Ariel, Chris ordered his crews to take rest and refreshment. There was no knowing what demands might be made of them in a few hours' time. Colin Johnson in Alpha and Tony in Beta kept up a desultory exchange of messages with Vari, but couldn't make anything more of them.

"I think we've gone to the limit of mutual understanding until we come face to face with him," Tony sighed. He wished very much that his ship had been selected to make the landing.

Ariel circles its primary at an average distance of 119,-000 miles from the center of Uranus. As the planet is 32,000 miles in diameter, Ariel is actually a little over 100,-000 miles above the surface. This would be close enough to gather a great deal of information about the huge planet—if Vari let them!

Three hours later Ariel had grown to the size of an orange when viewed through the observation ports. Alpha's telescope had revealed the same pitted surface that is characteristic of almost every airless body in the solar system. Chris studied the craters and mountains very carefully in a vain attempt to detect some sign of Vari.

"We probably won't spot him until we go into orbit round Ariel," Chris said at last. Originally he'd planned a straight run in for his ship, but now he'd decided that he must circle the satellite for a time before venturing down for a landing. This would let him pinpoint Vari's exact position. It would also show whether the alien had the power or the wish to be hostile at this distance. Though Chris was fairly confident that Vari would do them no harm, his duty to his companions required that he should take no undue risks.

"Everyone feel fit?" Chris asked his own crew and the crew of Beta. He was greeted with an affirmative chorus, for all the astronauts were eager to press on with their task.

The transfer into orbit around Ariel would have been a fairly simple exercise but for the tremendous attraction of

Uranus. It was necessary to have just the correct velocity and direction if the ships were to avoid being pulled into the giant planet. The on-board computer had calculated the details of the maneuver. Could the crews carry out this very critical operation?

It was now that the skills of Morrey and Serge, at the controls of their respective ships, were crucial. Chris had every confidence in his captains' experience and ability. But they were facing a novel situation. They were trying to get into orbit around a moon which housed a creature that might—or might not—have the power to influence their course. And always there would be Uranus waiting to drag them down into its own poisonous atmosphere.

There was almost complete silence in the two ships as the delicate maneuver was started. Only an occasional order from Morrey or Serge to another crewman broke the quiet. At last there was a long sigh of relief from Morrey.

"That's it!" he declared. The two ships were well and truly in orbit around the Uranian moon.

In contrast to the silence and apparent inactivity of a few moments before, the cabins of Alpha and Beta were now full of sound and movement. The crews set about observing Ariel, measuring their orbits, and trying to spot Vari.

"It's like the twin brother of our Moon," Robert Campbell declared after a spell at the observation port.

"It is also like Io, Ganymede, and Titan," Mervyn Williams said loftily, naming similar moons around other planets.

"And how many have you observed?" Robert demanded.

"That is nothing to do with it," the Welshman countered. "But what I say is right, is it not, Morrey?"

"I expect so," the American sighed, "but get on with your jobs, will you?"

Some 140 miles away, the surface of Ariel could be seen.

As the ships circled the satellite, it seemed as if they were motionless, and that it was Ariel that was turning beneath them. Only when Uranus, now seen as a brightly lighted semicircle, rose above the horizon did they get any impression of their own movement. Then the giant planet, with its half-open eye, seemed to be watching them balefully.

But where was Vari? His signals had faded and disappeared, showing that the two ships were now on the opposite side of Ariel. Both crews listened eagerly for their reappearance, as this would help to reveal just where the alien broadcaster was situated.

As the Uranian moon turned beneath them like an ever-moving carpet, the astronauts saw more and more features with which they were familiar on Earth's moon. There was the same litter of craters of all sizes. There were the flat plains and mountain ranges. There were cracks and faults very much as on our own Moon. And all these were in different shades of brown or gray.

"Got him!" shouted Colin in Alpha and Tony in Beta almost at the same time.

The Morse signals sent out by Vari were coming through in increasing strength, and Tony prepared to operate his direction finder.

"It looks as if he's somewhere in the region of that chain of craters coming into view now," Tony reported to Chris. "I think we'll pass over to the right of them."

"We can alter the orbit next time," Chris radioed back. "Let's make sure where he is for the moment."

A chain of four craters was steadily moving down the left of the spaceships' field of vision. All the astronauts who were not occupied crowded round the observation ports and looked at the craters curiously. If Tony was right, somewhere in one of those vast depressions a creature from another world was sending messages to them!

More and more they felt that Chris was right when he

guessed that the broadcaster had come from outside the solar system. He was now—either by design or accident— on barren, airless Ariel, but it was certain that Ariel itself couldn't have produced him. There was no sign of life on its frozen wastes. Had there been cities or some other products of civilization, they could have seen them even from this height.

So in which one of the four craters was Vari? All eyes were directed toward them, but they saw nothing.

"We'll alter course to pass overhead next time," Chris announced. "Get the telescope ready, Robert."

It took only a small burst to alter the course of the two ships. On their next orbit they should pass directly over the four craters. Robert had the telescope ready just as the line of depressions was appearing for a second time over Ariel's horizon. Chris took over and peered tensely through the instrument.

He was familiar with hundreds of lunar craters, and most of them had a small mountain in the center. Also he'd explored many of the Martian craters, which didn't have a central peak or such steep rims. These craters on Ariel were similar to the Martian ones, though perhaps some-what deeper. Chris scanned each of the four craters in turn, hoping to pick out anything unusual that might give a clue to Vari's position. It was in the last crater that he fancied he saw something. However, they had passed over it by that time, and would have to await the next orbit.

"Stay where you are," Chris ordered Beta. "I'm going down a little closer."

Handling the control of the spaceship expertly, he took Alpha down to within just under a hundred miles of the surface. He didn't want to get too close until he'd made sure just where the alien was. This time he concentrated on the crater where he thought he'd seen something unusual.

"See anything?" the voice of Tony demanded.

"Shut up a bit. We'll let you know as soon as we do," Morrey replied sharply. He didn't want to upset Chris's concentration on his vital task.

"Come and have a look," Chris called, and Morrey took his place at the eyepiece.

In the crater, not far from the top edge, a point of light shone. From nowhere else on the surface of Ariel had they seen reflected light. The rocky terrain would absorb rather than turn back the rays of the distant Sun. To see this shining point was most unusual. Coupled with Tony's pronouncement that he was now certain the signals were coming from the same crater, it seemed certain proof that they had finally tracked down the position of the broadcaster.

Each time the ships had passed over the four craters, the Morse signals had been loud and rapid.

"Perhaps he's spotted us and is getting excited about it," suggested Colin Johnson.

"He wouldn't if he knew what you are like," snorted Norman.

Chris had, of course, kept Control fully informed of their discoveries and the action he proposed to take. So far Control had not come up with any suggestions as to how the astronauts could increase their understanding of Vari's signals. Neither had they said how the crews could give the alien more information about themselves and their objective.

This threw a heavy responsibility onto Chris, and he felt it keenly. It would be his task and duty to establish the first direct contact between the human race and a creature from another world. Moreover, the contact could well decide the future relationship between the two. A false move by the leader of the expedition, a hasty judgment or the slightest impatience could well set the representatives of the two races against each other. While Chris didn't think

73

for a moment that Vari was hostile, he couldn't be sure. It would be so easy to turn mutual curiosity into animosity. And once that happened, the damage could well be irreparable.

"I'm going to land," Chris informed Serge, circling way up in Beta. "Keep in touch with us as long as you can."

The two ships would lose radio contact each time Beta disappeared over the horizon. Then, if Alpha wanted help, Chris would have to wait thirty-five minutes before the sister ship appeared again. He and his crew would be on their own during this period, away from all human contact and help. It was a disturbing thought.

"Good luck!" Serge called back. "Let us know if you want us to join you."

He almost said "if you want us to rescue you," but he concealed his fears. Alpha would make one more circuit to lose height, and then she would touch down in the nameless crater that seemed to be the home of the strange being from outer space.

Chris, his face tense with strain and concentration, began the final maneuver.

9

Now, though lord benson was no longer directing the operation, he had to give vent to his feelings somehow. So he scurried perpetually between the banks of instruments recording the flight of the two ships. As for Sir Billy, he was following reports of events with concentrated attention. He knew that all the information reaching Control was nearly three hours late. Much could have happened to the ships and their crews by the time signals could reach Earth. More than ever before the ultimate decisions had to be left with the expedition's commander. Control was largely a distant spectator.

The fact that the signals from the alien had now been changed to Morse made things much easier. Chris's vocal reports were much fuller. Even Control's replies were less terse than they would have been in Morse. Moreover, the voices of the distant astronauts conveyed something no Morse signal could have indicated—the growing tension and excitement of the crews as they saw their objective in sight.

For a fleeting moment, after Chris had reported the definite location of the broadcaster, Sir Billy felt a shiver of apprehension. There was time to call the whole thing off and recall the ships back to Earth. If he'd sent out such an order, he could well imagine how it would disappoint the astronauts. Yet he knew it would be obeyed, and the ships would scurry back home. However, this would only postpone the historic moment. Sooner or later, if not this year, then within a few years, man would make contact with another race. Now that it had been established beyond reasonable doubt that another race did exist, a meeting had become inevitable.

Lord Benson remembered very vividly the tremendous moment when a human foot first stepped onto the Moon. Since he'd retired, the former director had had a great deal of time to think, and he had become convinced that man was unconsciously following a fundamental urge—to seek out and to meet other intelligent races.

Chris's last message had said that they had pinpointed an object which he thought might be Vari and that he was going to set Alpha down alongside him. Preparations were going ahead in Control for the reception of television pictures, which were perhaps even now on their way across space. If they could discount a time lag of nearly three hours between an event on Ariel and the picture reaching the screens in Control, the staff at the Cape could feel that they were participating in the encounter. Though they were separated by so many millions of miles, Sir Billy and his men felt the same tense anticipation as the astronauts.

The first flicker on the television screens caused a ripple of excitement among all those who could spare the time to watch. Sir Billy and Lord Benson hurried to the monitor on the director's desk. As yet there was little to see. Vaguely, one got the impression of something moving.

"They're scanning the surface," Sir Billy said after a few moments' close attention. "If they would hold still for a few seconds, we could improve the picture."

As if the distant astronauts had heard his words, the picture on the television screens remained static. Sir Billy pointed out the Moonlike features that Chris had described, and gradually, as the picture improved, everyone in Control was able to pick out the pattern of craters, hills, and mountains. Chris's voice was giving a commentary on the scene, and when he said that the crater in which Vari was lurking was coming up, everyone crowded round the screens.

"That's the one," Chris told them, and Billy and Lord Benson picked out the row of four circular depressions coming into view.

It was the right-hand one that drew all the attention, for, according to Chris, this was the home of the alien. Yet, in spite of the closest scrutiny, they could detect nothing unusual.

"Probably too small for us to pick out," the director breathed. "Maybe we'll get it on the next orbit."

Chris hadn't said how many orbits round the satellite he would make in spiraling down. If Lord Benson knew anything of his favorite astronaut, Chris would control his natural eagerness to land. He would approach the strange broadcaster cautiously. Each time Alpha passed over Vari's crater, it would be nearer the surface. The crew would be on the alert for any reaction.

The crew in Beta were anxiously following their friends' progress. It was most exasperating that the two ships were in radio contact only for brief spells. Tony was for plying Alpha with a string of questions, but Serge told him to keep quiet and to leave the radio link open to Chris.

"Height, ten miles," Chris called. "Am touching down in two minutes."

This meant that Alpha was now making its approach run. Its altitude had been reduced so that when the four craters next appeared on the horizon, Chris would cut down the forward speed and pick out his landing point, unless he saw something that made him change his mind at the last minute. The ship had an ample reserve of fuel, and could alter course many times. But astronauts had developed a professional pride in putting down their ships when they

77

wanted and where they wanted. Chris planned a clear-cut maneuver to set Alpha on the ground.

Ah! Here the four craters came now, with the ship heading for the one on the right. From this altitude they looked much larger, and two of the craters moved quickly off the screen. All the attention of the crew was directed to their landing point—and to looking to see what Vari was really like.

Because the sun's rays now came from a different direction, nothing was reflected to them from inside the crater.

"So it was reflected light," Colin ventured.

No one replied, for everyone was too wrapped up in his job. It was Norman Spier who spotted the object on the ground.

"Looks like a ship!" he burst out.

There, directly in their path and obviously the only possible object that could have sent out radio signals, was a huge, strange-looking spaceship.

At least, Chris guessed that it must be a spaceship, though to human eyes it seemed extraordinary. Instead of the cylindrical or spherical basic shape of man-made spaceships, this one was completely irregular. It had bulges and lumps in many places, even sharp points sticking up. It had no sign of hatch or porthole and seemed to be of a dull, yellowish color. Only the contrast with the surrounding terrain showed that this ungainly shape was no part of Ariel.

As Alpha drew nearer and sank lower, the strange object could be seen to glisten. As the rays of the distant Sun caught certain parts, they reflected the light, and it was this that had first caught the astronauts' attention up in orbit.

Vari was transmitting strongly, but apart from his own name and that of the two ships, his message was unintelligible. Chris would have given a great deal to understand what the signals meant. That the alien hadn't reverted to his original distressing signals might show that he was not hostile, but it would need a close inspection and an actual encounter to put this beyond doubt.

In spite of a close scrutiny, none of Alpha's crew could detect any familiar features in the strange ship below them. There was no sign of any radio antenna or even of any form of propulsion. It seemed to be lying there—just a squat, ugly, artificial feature.

Chris took a deep breath as he began the final procedure for landing. While Morrey's quiet voice in the background was giving a commentary for the benefit of Beta and Control, the leader manipulated his rockets for the touchdown. Norman and Colin were at the radar, calling out height and distance.

"Seven hundred and fifty feet," called Norman.

"Eighteen miles," intoned Colin.

A little burst nudged Alpha along. Another checked the rate of fall. The crater walls were very near now, and Chris was looking anxiously at the surface within them. It would be essential to choose a flat area to land on, for if the ship settled on a slope or a lump of rock, it could well fall over and be incapable of ever returning to Earth.

It was as if Vari, too, had obligingly chosen a landing spot that would help them. The alien spacecraft—if that is what it was—was parked on a flat area surrounded by rock-strewn terrain. But within a hundred yards or so was another flat area, an ideal spot on which to settle the ship.

Without hesitation Chris headed toward this plain, relieved that he'd discovered an area so flat and so close to their objective. He told his crew of his decision to land here, and all attention was focused on the place indicated.

"One hundred and fifty feet," Norman called out, a note of rising excitement in his voice.

"Two miles," Colin called back, equally excited.

Morrey, too, was talking more rapidly into the microphone. Only Chris, it seemed, was unaffected.

However, this wasn't quite true. He was feeling the same excitement as his companions, but concentration on his task and a determination to let nothing impair his cool judgment enabled him to keep his feelings under strict control. Not even the nearness of the strange Thing on the neighboring landing ground distracted his attention.

"Forty-eight feet."

"One thousand yards."

And the crew were holding their breaths. Nearer. Nearer. Legs out! That's it. Bump!

At the last moment Chris had extended the retractable landing legs. They had touched, and Alpha had landed!

There was an immediate relaxation of tension in the cabin. A touchdown always gave rise to it, particularly when it was on a new and unknown surface. Would Alpha tilt or sink? The ship remained steadfastly upright.

It had been strictly laid down that when a landing was made, there must be no attempt to open the hatch until at least an hour had passed. This was to enable the ship and the ground to cool off and to give the crew an opportunity to make preliminary observations. Naturally, most of that hour was spent by the astronauts in crowding round the portholes and watching intently the strange shape only a hundred yards away.

"He's stopped transmitting," Colin announced.

He'd switched on the radio that was tuned in to Vari's wavelength, but it remained silent. Was this a good sign or a bad one? It could only mean that the alien was aware that they had landed.

"Try calling him," Chris suggested, but there was no response.

"I hope nothing has happened just as we've arrived," Norman Spier said doubtfully. "It would be an anticlimax if our journey had been wasted."

"I don't think you need fear that," Chris assured him. "We're going to have a closer look at this spaceship, or whatever it is."

The object of their inspection had remained completely unchanged since the crew had been scrutinizing it. The occasional sparkle from the otherwise dull-yellow mass indicated that the ship might be made of some crystalline substance. None of the astronauts could recall having seen anything like it before. Certainly no spaceship they knew was made of such material.

"This is my plan," Chris said to his crew. "In fifteen minutes' time Norman and I will leave Alpha, and go and inspect the alien ship. The moment we reach the ground, you are to seal the hatch and be ready to blast off at a second's notice. If anything happens, there must be no heroics, no attempt to help us. Your plain duty is to get away and report to Control."

"But, Chris, we couldn't leave you behind," protested Colin.

"You could—and you must," the leader said firmly. "In case I can't give the order later, I'll give it to you now. At the slightest sign of hostile action by Vari, you must take off and join Beta. You can then all consult together as to your next step. There's no need for me to remind you that your paramount duty is to avoid risks and to get back to Earth with our observations."

There was no room for argument. The others could see by the firm line of Chris's jaw that he would tolerate none. Both Morrey and Colin would dearly have loved to be the first to make contact with the intelligent creature within the foreign spaceship. Yet they recognized how foolish it would be for all four astronauts to venture from the protection of Alpha before they were certain that Vari would do them no harm.

"Let's suit up," Chris said briskly to Norman.

The two men, assisted by Morrey and Colin, donned

their suits in silence. They were wondering what the next hour would bring. Would it end in their annihilation? Or would it be one of the most tremendous moments in human history?

At last the hour had elapsed, the ship and the ground had cooled, and Chris and Norman stood by the airlock. A last-minute test confirmed that their helmet radios were both working, so they would be in constant contact with their companions sealed in Alpha.

"Let's go," Chris said over his radio, and he stepped toward the airlock.

This small compartment could only take one astronaut at a time. To save precious oxygen, the air had to be pumped out before the outer hatch was opened. This only took a few seconds, and soon a red light shone in the airlock, telling Chris that all was now ready for him to open the door and to face the unknown waiting outside.

"Here goes," the others heard him say. "I'm opening the hatch now. It's open."

There was a pause while the leader surveyed his surroundings before climbing down the ladder to the surface.

"It's just like the Moon," he said.

But the Moon hadn't an intelligent creature from another world waiting just a hundred yards away!

10

CHRIS GLANCED DOWN. Under earthly gravity Alpha weighed more than a hundred tons, but on this small satellite its weight would be less than one-tenth of that. Even so, it was important to see what impression the landing legs had made. This would give the astronaut his first clue as to the nature of the surface on which he must walk.

The huge spring-loaded pads on the end of each foot seemed to have made little mark on the rocklike surface. The blast from the rocket motor had seared the area for twenty yards around, but the ground beneath him seemed firm enough. Carefully, one foot after another, Chris climbed down the ladder until a foot touched the rock. Then he stood—the first human to do so—on the Uranian moon.

"Surface okay," he called back over his radio. Then he took a few careful steps away from the ladder to await the descent of Norman. In a few seconds the airlock door opened, and a space-suited figure began to clamber down. Soon the two astronauts stood together in the shadow of their ship.

The scene was one of utter desolation. Where the flame of the rocket had scorched the rock, it was a dark brown and had a glossy appearance. Any loose stones had been swept away, and Chris could see a ring of small rocks surrounding their landing point. Farther out was the jumble of boulders and small craters that they had observed during the descent.

Alpha and every other projection were casting two shadows, one from the brilliant point of light that was the Sun, and a less intense one from the giant Uranus now filling a quarter of the sky.

It was very tempting to stand and stare at the scene around them or to look with wonder at the cloud-covered giant that was creeping up the sky. But the astronauts had a more pressing and dangerous task. They must walk on and encounter the alien creature that was awaiting them a hundred yards away.

Vari was still silent. For some time now no signals had come from the unearthly spaceship. Was this a good sign or not? The next few minutes would decide.

"Are you okay outside?" the anxious voice of Morrey asked.

"We're fine," Chris assured him. "We're off now to meet our friend—I hope."

He stepped out and was soon beyond the area cleared by the rocket. Then the astronauts began to pick their way carefully between the boulders of all sizes that were strewn in all directions. Great care was necessary, for a fall or a cut in one of their boots by a sharp rock could be disastrous. In the high vacuum and intense frost of Ariel, even the smallest puncture in their protective clothing could have the most harmful results.

Once Norman stepped on a small rock that rolled from beneath his foot. As he stumbled, Chris grabbed him and saved him from the fall. There were plenty of jagged pieces of rock about awaiting to bring disaster. After that the astronauts proceeded with extreme caution. Five minutes' careful walk brought them to the end of the rock ground, and to the smooth area beyond. And there, before their eyes, lay the spaceship from beyond the solar system!

"It's about a hundred yards across," Chris began his description. "There seems to be a huge, bulbous nose at one end, and all sorts of odd curves and shapes. It has a sharp ridge along the top, almost like a spine. I can't see any porthole or hatch."

There was only one thing to do—to walk round the ship and look at it from all sides. Keeping the same distance from their objective, Chris and Norman plodded along a circular path until they had gone completely round their objective. The same unbroken surface, with an occasional patch glistening in the sun, met them from all sides.

"Can't see a thing," Chris radioed back to Alpha. Yet they were confident that within that peculiar shape lurked Something that had sent intelligent messages back to them —Something that knew the science of numbers and had an advanced radio technique.

"I'll go up and take a closer look," Norman said.

"You most certainly will not," Chris replied firmly. "You will stay right here for a few moments while I go. I'll call you in if I find anything."

Norman knew it was no use protesting. Chris always undertook the most dangerous parts of any mission himself. This had caused endless arguments with his crews in the past. In vain they had protested that Chris was the most valuable man in the expedition—that it was more important that he should survive than anyone else. Chris was deaf to all these arguments, merely replying that the safety of his colleagues was his responsibility and that he was going to test that safety first.

Aware of the significance of the moment, Chris stepped resolutely toward the unfamiliar mass. The ground was smooth, and as he walked forward, the trained astronaut in him noted automatically that there was no scorching of the rock as their own spaceship had caused upon landing. The occasional small loose pebbles also indicated that the

85

area had not been blasted clear by any rocket exhaust. He reached the alien spaceship without incident.

It would have seemed natural to call out, "Is anyone there?" But even if the surrounding vacuum hadn't made such a thing impossible, Vari could not have understood.

Was the alien aware of Chris's presence? There was no indication that he was, so Chris began to examine the outside of the ship minutely.

It was certainly an artificial structure. He could see the crystalline nature of the walls, and it was completely unlike any metal or mineral that he knew on Earth. He tapped it experimentally with his gloved hand.

He was puzzled. How could he make contact with this Creature from another world if it remained locked in a spaceship with no doors or windows? Should he beat a Morse tattoo on the side? Even if he did, he could not hear if there was any response.

"Call him up again on the radio," Chris ordered his friends back in Alpha. Yet how could they tell Vari that his visitors were outside when they didn't speak his language and had no idea what form it took? Nevertheless, Colin tapped away a message, constantly spelling out "Vari" and "Alpha." There was no response.

"Can I come alongside?" the plaintive voice of Norman sounded over Chris's radio. For a moment the leader had forgotten his companion waiting patiently on the edge of the flat area.

"Yes, come along," he replied, "but there's nothing to see."

Without waiting for Chris to change his mind, Norman hurried forward to join him. And then the accident happened. In his rush to get to the strange spaceship, Norman trod carelessly on a pebble. It was quite small, but it was sufficient to make him lose his footing. He fell, and his space helmet struck the alien vessel. Then he lay quite still.

Out of the corner of his eye Chris had seen what happened, and he was filled with alarm. If the bump had caused the slightest fracture in Norman's helmet, all his oxygen would be sucked out, and he would be dead in a few seconds. There would be nothing Chris could do to save him. There wouldn't be time to carry him back to Alpha. He would die alongside the alien that they had traveled so many millions of miles to meet.

Chris bent over him. Through the visor he could see Norman's pale face and closed eyes. Then Chris's heart gave a great leap of relief. The astronaut's features were not swollen, as they would have been if the pressure in his helmet had fallen to the same as the surrounding vacuum.

As carefully as he could, Chris examined his friend's equipment. It was difficult in his space suit, but he managed to do it fairly thoroughly. There was no sign of a fracture in the helmet or a cut in any part of the suit. Maybe Norman had just knocked himself unconscious. There was no way Chris could tell.

He reported back to Alpha and asked Colin to come out and join him. They would have to get Norman back to the ship before they did anything else. Chris could have carried him alone, but it would be better to have help in transporting him across the rough ground.

Quite oblivious now of the strange spaceship beside him and of the creature it housed, Chris gave all his attention to Norman. It was impossible to feel his pulse, of course, or to detect if he was breathing. Until help came, he could only look into his visor.

From time to time Chris glanced anxiously back toward Alpha. How quickly could Colin put on his suit and make his way to them? Several times Chris was tempted to take the great risk of trying to carry Norman himself, but a moment's reflection convinced him that he stood little chance of hauling his friend across the rocky ground without help. He could easily become a casualty himself, and that would complicate matters immeasurably.

Ah! The airlock door had opened, and someone was clambering down the ladder.

"I'm on my way," the voice of Colin Johnson announced over Chris's helmet radio.

"Good. Take care, though," Chris called back.

He glanced down again at the still figure and put his visor close to Norman's. Then his heart gave a leap, for the astronaut was regaining consciousness. First his eyes began to flicker, and then they opened. As he regained his senses, Norman managed a wan smile at Chris. He began to struggle to get to his feet.

"Easy now," Chris commanded. "You stay there awhile. You've had a nasty crack."

"What—what happened?" Norman gasped.

"You stumbled and hit your head against our alien friend's abode," Chris informed him. "You've been out for about ten minutes."

A look of apprehension crossed Norman's face. "Has there been any sign of—of *him?*" he asked.

"None," his leader assured him. "Not a sound or sign. Colin is on his way over to help me get you back to the ship."

"I'll be all right," Norman insisted, again attempting to rise. Chris gently pushed him back.

"We're going to get you back to the ship to see what damage it's done to you and to the helmet," the leader said firmly.

"Where's the patient?" Colin asked as he arrived.

"I'm no patient," Norman protested, "but Chris wants to mollycoddle me."

"Help me to get him up," Chris ordered. "We'll take him back and have a look at the damage." He could see a trickle of blood running down Norman's face.

As Chris and Colin helped Norman to his feet, he again insisted that he could walk.

"All right," agreed Chris, "but we're going to grab your ams." He didn't want Norman to faint or stumble again.

"You should have let me come with you, Chris," Colin said cheerfully as the three began their walk back to Alpha. "At least my head is well protected."

"Your skull is certainly thick, if that's what you mean," Norman retorted.

"No thicker than yours," Colin retaliated, "but at least I can grow hair."

"Look where you're going," Chris commanded sternly, but he was glad his companions were in good spirits.

They picked their way carefully to Alpha, where Morrey was waiting for their return. Norman was sent through the airlock first, and even before the other two were inside, Morrey had removed Norman's helmet to examine the damage.

He had a nasty cut just over his right ear, and it was oozing blood. With expert hands, Morrey disinfected it, an important precaution in this strange environment. Then he pulled the wound together and covered it with a plaster from the ship's first-aid kit. Chris and Colin inspected the patient as soon as their helmets were off.

"How do you feel?" Chris asked. "A bit shaken?"

"Just a bit. Otherwise I'm fine," Norman declared stoutly. "I'll have a drink, then we'll start back."

"Not on your life," Chris said firmly. "You'll stay inside the ship and rest. Colin, you have your suit on. You can come back with me."

The long-haired astronaut couldn't help giving a triumphant grin at his bald colleague, but he refrained from saying anything.

"Perhaps we'll all have some refreshment," Morrey suggested. "Do you want to change your oxygen bottles?"

"Good idea," Chris agreed. "I'll send in a report meanwhile. Although as far as Vari is concerned, there's nothing to report. Is Beta in range?"

"Just about," Morrey answered, "but you'll have to be quick."

In a few minutes their sister ship would sink below Ariel's horizon and would be out of radio range until it reappeared circling the satellite's far side. Chris spoke quickly into the microphone and was able to put Serge into the picture. In turn the Russian reported that nothing important had come in from Control meanwhile.

"Right. We're on our way back again," Chris told him. "We hope to have some news for you when you come back."

Colin was waiting, all eager to venture out onto the barren surface. He led the way down the ladder and stood awaiting his leader.

"I've been thinking," Chris said as they made their way carefully toward the peculiar ship. "We'll examine the surface all over very carefully. It may be difficult to find a door or hatch, but there's bound to be one somewhere. We may have to climb on top if you're game."

"Suits me fine," Colin radioed back. "I've brought a small torch with me."

He was referring to a laser gun, a piece of electrical equipment that astronauts used to cut off small samples of rock or metal. It was used extensively when exploring new territory, and even if the alien spaceship hadn't been present, the crew would have wanted it to take samples of Ariel's material.

"I don't think we'd better use that on the ship," Chris said doubtfully, "at least not for the present. Let's see what we can find out from a closer inspection."

This time both astronauts walked right up to the intruder and right round it, scrutinizing it carefully.

"Can't see a thing," Colin declared. "Shall I have a look on top?"

"No. Help me up," the leader answered, and he smiled to himself at Colin's audible snort of disgust.

Very gingerly, though it wasn't difficult under Ariel's low gravity, Chris climbed up the spaceship's side with Colin's help. He'd chosen a part behind one of the bulges, where the ship was about twelve feet high. He was about to grab the "spine" and haul himself up to sit astride it, when the most astounding thing that had ever happened in the lives of any of the astronauts occurred.

A voice spoke over their radios! A voice that spoke their own language! A voice that belonged to none of them, to no human being!

Vari was speaking!

11

"CHRIS AND COLIN," the voice said, "wait a little, and I will let you in."

The words were heard plainly not only by the two astronauts near the alien spaceship, but also by the pair listening in Alpha. Beta was, of course, out of range. At once there was dead silence. Chris froze into immobility where he sat. Colin stood as if turned into a statue. In Alpha, Morrey and Norman grew pale as they guessed what was happening. Contact had been made.

It was Chris who forced himself to speak first.

"Wh—who are you?" he stammered.

The voice—they found it quite a pleasant one—spoke again.

"I am a being from a distant world. I am he whom I have heard you call Vari," it said.

"But you can speak! You can speak English!" Chris burst out.

"I will explain all to you in good time," the voice of Vari said. "Now please do not be at all alarmed. I am a friend."

"Are—are you inside this ship?" Colin managed to squeak.

"Yes, and you may come inside soon. But first there is much that we must talk about. You are the first creatures of the planet Earth to meet someone from elsewhere. I must be sure that you can stand the shock."

Chris very carefully eased himself off the spaceship and joined Colin. In an unconscious gesture the two Earthmen held gloved hands. It was as if they were giving each other mutual support to face this stupefying situation. Their training hadn't prepared them for it. Now they must depend on their natural courage.

"Let's—let's get back to Alpha," Colin gasped.

This was Chris's reaction too. But they had come many millions of miles to make this encounter. It was the main reason for the expedition. They couldn't run away now.

"I have said you need have no fear," the voice of Vari said. "A meeting like this must happen sometime. It has been inevitable since life first began on your planet."

"But—how is it that you can speak English?" Chris forced himself to ask. "Why haven't you spoken before?"

"You will have many questions to ask me. I will answer all I can, but there are many things that you would not understand. For the moment I will tell you that we have listened to all the broadcasts from Earth since you discovered radio. We could have learned your language from that. You may accept that explanation for the moment."

"Yes, but why did you send those uncomfortable radio signals to Earth? Why did you transmit to us in Morse instead of talking to us?" Chris persisted.

"Can you not imagine what the reaction would have been among your race if we had spoken directly to them? It would have been scarcely less frightening than if I had arrived on Earth myself. So it was with you. I signaled to you in Morse to prepare you gradually for this encounter," Vari explained.

"I don't think we would have been all that scared," protested Chris. "We thought this might happen sometime. We have thought a lot about it."

93

"'Thinking about it' and 'reality' are two different things," Vari insisted patiently. "It is true that in some measure your people have been prepared for our meeting by some of your writings. Science fiction, I believe you call them. But these have only been stories culled from the imagination of the authors. Even with their help your people could not have survived the shock of meeting us. So we have worked out a careful plan about how to introduce ourselves to you."

"I must report to Earth," Chris burst out. "Morrey, have you heard all this?"

"Yes," the strained voice of the American came back. "Shall I pass everything on to Control?"

"Forgive me, my friends," the voice of Vari broke in. "It is inadvisable to announce me in that way. Therefore I have stopped your communicating with your people for the moment. I have put a screen round this satellite that your radio waves cannot penetrate. I will remove it again later."

"So that's why we're not getting anything from Control," Morrey cut in. "Yet we can still speak to Beta—or could before it went out of range."

"My screen is beyond the orbit of your other ship," the alien explained. "You will be able to speak to your friends when they next appear. But neither they nor you can send radio signals back to your people."

"That's a rotten trick," Norman's voice declared indignantly. "Take your screen away at once."

"Not yet but soon," Vari promised. "Believe me, my friends, this is necessary for the moment."

"You still haven't said why you sent those harmful signals—if, as you say, you wish us no ill," Chris pointed out.

"The signals would have caused you no permanent harm," Vari said patiently. "We had to use them to per-

94

suade you to send an expedition to their source. We knew that you were able to do so, but it might have been many of your years before you came to these outer reaches of your system."

"Maybe so, but why did you want to make us come now?" inquired Colin, who seemed to be recovering from his first shock.

"There is a reason, which you will learn in due time," the alien replied.

"What are you like?" Colin asked. "Are you like us?"

"My race has many forms," Vari said. "I was sent to meet you because I am almost like you. This will make our meeting easier. Some of the forms my people take cannot be described in your language."

"Well, when are we going to meet you?" Colin asked. He seemed anxious to wipe out the memory of his wish to run away.

"Perhaps you would care to invite your friends in your ship to join you," Vari suggested. "Then you could all meet me together. Would you also like to call down your other ship the next time it passes over?"

Chris didn't think he was suspicious by nature. He preferred to think that it was his ingrained sense of caution that made him hesitate. Vari sounded friendly enough, and his actions to date had been logical and reasonable. But Chris wasn't yet entirely sure about him.

The alien had answered their questions, but there were innumerable others that still had to be asked. Until Chris knew more answers than he did now, he wasn't going to call all his colleagues to meet Vari at the same time. If Colin and he fared well, there would be plenty of time for the other six to meet this man from another world.

Man? Vari had said that he'd been selected to make the first contact with humans, for he was somewhat like them. Chris conceded that it would be much easier to establish

95

an understanding with a creature very similar to himself than with something as grotesque as the creatures in some of the stories he'd read.

"My crew will all remain where they are for the moment," he told Vari. "Colin and I will meet you first."

"As you wish," the alien replied. Did Chris detect a note of disappointment in his voice?

"Beta will soon be in range," the voice of Morrey said. "Any instructions?"

"No. Just put them in the picture and tell them to carry on. No doubt they've been wondering what's happened to Control," Chris replied.

"When you are inside the ship, you will not touch anything," Vari said. "This is because you will not understand much that you see. You could harm yourselves if you do not follow my instructions."

"Very well," Chris agreed, "but tell us where your hatch is. We haven't seen one."

"There is no opening to this ship, at least not one as you know it. What you—"

"How can we come inside if there's no entrance?" Colin burst out, unable to contain his amazement.

"Patience, my friend," Vari advised. "I was just about to explain to you. Technology has advanced far beyond your conception, far beyond the need to have a mechanical entrance, as your ships have. You simply walk through my ship's wall."

"But—but that's impossible," Chris gasped. "Your ship is made of something—I don't know what it is—that is very solid and strong. How can we walk through the outer casing?"

"I will give you a first glimpse of our technology," the alien's voice said with the hint of a smile in it. "Everything that looks solid is, as I'm sure you know, made up of molecules of different materials. Molecules are, in turn, made

96

from the atoms of elements, and the atoms consist of nuclei surrounded by clouds of electrons. Far from matter being solid, it consists mainly of open space.

"You have circled this satellite and you know the size as it is now. If all the matter in it were to be compressed until there was no space left within it, the size would be no larger than my ship. Every cubic foot would weigh millions of tons. So you see, neither my ship, nor you, are really solid. There is plenty of space for your atoms to pass between the ship's atoms when you come inside."

"But that's impossible," the voice of Norman Spier interrupted. "Why didn't Chris fall into your ship when he was sitting on top? Why is it that when we touched your ship our hands didn't pass through the side?"

"It requires the setting up of an electrical field," Vari explained. "This aligns the atoms so that they can pass through each other. When you are ready to enter my ship, I will set up such a field and so enable you to walk through the walls. Are you ready?"

"Why don't you come out here to meet us?" Chris wanted to know.

"As I have explained to you, I am very much like you. And like you, I need oxygen to breathe. I would have to put on what you call a space suit if I venture outside to meet you. Would you not prefer to see me as I am, and to see what my ship is like?" the alien asked.

"Fair enough," Chris conceded. "What do you want us to do?"

"Stay where you are while I set up the electrical field. When I tell you, just walk into the ship as if the walls did not exist," he was told.

Even now neither of the astronauts could believe that what Vari had said was possible. It was contrary to all human experience. Walking through a solid structure as if it didn't exist! Colin was confident that they would bang

97

themselves on the ship's wall. And what fools they would look!

Chris's mind was racing in another direction. If Vari could do what he said, which he couldn't believe, and they found themselves inside the strange spaceship, what was to prevent the alien from turning off the electrical field and so making prisoners of them? Was he really friendly, or was he trying to deceive them? Was he a spider luring two human flies into his highly technical web?

Chris had to make the vital decision. As far as they knew, they were free to refuse Vari's invitation to walk into his ship. They were also free, so Chris believed, to return to Alpha and blast off from this queer creature. Should they now retreat with what dignity they could muster? Or should they accept the alien's declaration of friendship and enter his vessel?

If Vari was hostile, he could easily harm them. They had no doubt about the technical ability of this intruder into our solar system. Had he not already demonstrated his complete mastery of radio? The very presence of this strange vessel sitting quietly on Ariel was proof positive that Vari commanded fantastic resources. If he wished to stop them, any attempt to leave the satellite would be futile. He could probably put all the electrical apparatus aboard Alpha out of action. He could imprison them in their ship just as surely as he could in his own vessel. "We may as well put on a bold face," Chris decided.

"Beta is coming into range," Morrey suddenly called over the radio. The two astronauts about to meet the alien face to face, and their companions, tensely following events from inside Alpha, had almost forgotten the existence of their sister ship. Now that Beta was racing into radio range, its crew were firing questions at their companions on the ground.

"Does Chris want us to land?" Serge asked hopefully, but he was informed that their leader still insisted on the second ship's remaining aloft.

There were gasps from the crew of Beta as Morrey rapidly described what was about to happen to Chris and Colin. Because they knew that the alien would hear their conversation, Serge and his crew hesitated to advise caution to Chris. Though they were alarmed at the possible outcome, they had supreme confidence in the wisdom of their leader.

"I am about to set up the electrical field," Vari said, apparently ignoring the questions of Beta's crew. "If you feel any sensation, it will be a mild one and quite harmless. Remain where you are until I give the word. Then step inside."

"Step inside!" Wasn't this the invitation issued by the spider to the fly? Chris had to fight off his doubts. They were committed. They must enter this fantastic vessel.

A slight tingling sensation began to affect the two astronauts. It was nothing to worry about, but Colin looked quickly at Chris. After all, it was going to take all their courage to go through with this. A glance at his leader was necessary to give him just that extra touch of assurance.

In a few seconds' time, two tremendous events would be taking place. They were going to test whether or not two solid bodies could pass through each other. And they were going—assuming it did happen—to meet the strange creature who had brought it about.

The helmet radios had now fallen silent. Both Morrey and Norman, peering anxiously through Alpha's observation port, and the Beta crew were conscious of the situation. Neither dared speak at the moment. Neither had anything to say.

"Are you ready?" Vari asked.

The tingling seemed to have died down. Even as he was about to reply, Chris noticed that it went altogether. Presumably—if that was what was going to happen—all his atoms had been lined up in the right direction. Would he now shatter his visor against the solid ship, or would he perform a miracle?

"Yes, we're ready," Chris called back, trying to keep his voice calm.

"Very well," the alien replied. "Walk!"

12

Though everyone in Control knew that, by now, Alpha would have landed, the messages and pictures that were coming through were still of the last orbit and final approach to Vari's crater. Not until the ship was on its final run up did the scientists at Cape Kennedy get a glimpse of what might be an alien spaceship. Its strange shape and large size made it look like some prehistoric monster awaiting its prey.

"It's certainly never traveled in an atmosphere," was Lord Benson's opinion as he watched the moving picture. Everyone agreed that the ship, if that was what it was, had no aerodynamic shape. It would burn up from friction if it moved through an atmosphere at anything like high speed.

"That's if it's made from any materials that we know," Sir Billy agreed more cautiously. "It may be subject to physical laws that we don't yet know about."

They fell silent as they listened to the instrument readings of the distant spaceship.

"One hundred and fifty feet," one voice called out.

"Two miles," another came in, giving the height.

Morrison Kant, the second in command, was giving a running description of the final approach, and the rising excitement in his voice was perceptible even over these millions of miles. Lord Benson was gripping the arms of his chair until his knuckles went white. He was living every moment with his distant friends.

"We've landed."

Was it distance that distorted the fateful words? Or was it the intense excitement of the broadcaster? The listeners in Control gasped in sympathy.

Lord Benson's frustration was almost beyond endurance. More than anything he wanted to shout words of caution and encouragement to his young friends. But long before the radio waves could carry his voice to them, they would have left the spaceship and made their encounter with the alien. Even now some disaster might have overtaken them, while their voices were still being received by the anxious men at the Cape.

Sir Billy Gillanders, being directly responsible for the expedition, felt the same. Benson was mainly concerned with the safety of the astronauts, but the director carried the crushing burden of the whole undertaking. Not only must the eight young men return safely, they must discover what was happening on Ariel. They must find out if the signals really came from an intelligent creature from another solar system, and if so, they must lay the foundations for future contacts.

A hand fell on Lord Benson's shoulder, but it was some seconds before he could wrench his thoughts from the peril his friends were in. Then he looked up at the figure beside him. He nearly exploded.

"Whiskers!" he spluttered. "What brings you here?"

It was indeed his old friend and colleague "Whiskers" Greatrex, the ex-RAF officer with the vast moustache.

"I couldn't keep away," Whiskers confessed. "What's happening, Benny?"

Lord Benson knew that Whiskers had been very close to four of the astronauts who were now facing the most tremendous event of their lives. In his own words, he'd been a "nanny" to them before most of their space voyages. When they had landed on a distant planet and were in a position of some danger, it had been the cheerful voice of Whiskers coming over their radios that had kept up their spirits.

Though he now had no official status at Cape Kennedy, he was known to everyone and had had no difficulty in being admitted. It had been more than he could bear to remain aloof while Chris and his friends were undergoing this tremendous experience.

Lord Benson rapidly brought his old friend up to date, and the grin faded from beneath the famous moustache. Whiskers realized that Chris and the rest were up against a situation that no one had ever faced before, about which no guidance or advice could be given. It was even useless to try to cheer them up, for his jokes and banter would be as stale as last week's newspapers by the time his words reached them. Nevertheless, he wanted to send a message letting them know he was in Control.

Sir Billy took Whiskers over to the microphone and let him broadcast his message. Not for five and a half hours would a reply come back.

The loudspeaker was still reporting the words of Morrey, and occasionally from Tony in Beta. It seemed that Alpha was now waiting for the ground to cool, while her sister ship kept station up above the satellite.

Then the radio went dead. Quite suddenly the messages from both ships ceased. At first it was thought that a fault had developed in the receiver at Control, but in a few seconds the standby receiver was brought in—with the same result.

"Something's happened!" Sir Billy said. His face had suddenly become very drawn. Lord Benson began to shake, and Whiskers' face lost some of its ruddy color. He handed the microphone back to an engineer.

"What could it be?" he demanded.

"We don't know," Billy replied, struggling to keep calm. "Even if something has happened to the landing party, why aren't we getting something from the others safely in orbit?"

"Perhaps Beta has gone out of range," suggested Lord Benson.

"No. It wasn't due to move behind the satellite for another twenty minutes," the director said. "In fact, Tony's voice is the last sound we have recorded."

"Then it must be some electrical interference," Lord Benson asserted. "Even if harm has befallen Alpha and its crew—which God forbid—the four in Beta should be well out of harm's way. Is it possible that a radiation belt has moved between us?"

Such things did happen, though only very rarely. It would account for the complete blotting out of radio signals from both ships.

"Is there a sunspot?" Whiskers inquired.

This, too, might affect radio communication. All too often the appearance of a huge disturbance on the Sun's surface would cause radio signals throughout the solar system to be blotted out for a time.

"I'll check," Sir Billy promised, "but I think the answer will be no."

Gloom had fallen throughout that long room. All the men and women who were responsible for monitoring and controlling the expedition felt that something terrible had happened, something which, in spite of their sophisticated instruments and equipment, they were powerless to prevent. Not even the telemetry signals were getting through from either ship!

"No. No sunspot or radiation belt," Sir Billy announced as he returned to his two friends. "We're getting signals from Lunar City and all automatic stations. This seems to be a purely local blackout."

"Local to Uranus—or rather, Ariel?" Lord Benson asked.

"Seems like it," the director replied. "We're getting no trouble from anywhere else."

"Then that seems pretty conclusive," Benson said seriously. "The alien is hostile."

Strangely enough, it was Whiskers who broke the heavy silence.

"Oh, I wouldn't say that," he said quietly. "I'm sure there's some other explanation."

Because of their deep respect and affection for him, the two scientists didn't laugh. But they looked at him almost pityingly.

Whiskers flushed slightly as he interpreted their glances.

"Can we go somewhere to talk?" he asked. "There's something on my mind that I must get off. I can't do it here."

"Go to my office," Billy said. "I'll follow when I've given instructions to one or two section leaders. We must maintain constant radio watch."

Lord Benson led the way, and Whiskers strode along beside him, wondering if he had the moral courage to tell Benny and Billy what was in his mind.

"What's troubling you, Whiskers?" the director asked as he closed the door.

Poor Whiskers shuffled uncomfortably. He'd rather meet an enemy a hundred times than say what he had to to these two men. Still—he'd committed himself, and he couldn't draw back now.

"Well," he began. "I don't know how I'm going to say it, but let me ask you one thing first. Do you think I've gone soft in the head in my old age?"

Lord Benson and Sir Billy would have laughed aloud if they hadn't seen that his question was a serious one.

"You're as good as you ever were," Billy assured his friend heartily, "and as for age—well, you'll outlive me, I don't doubt."

"Of course you're all right," Lord Benson agreed. "I would say that you're more mature and balanced than when I first knew you."

"Thank goodness for that," Whiskers breathed, "for there have been times when I myself began to wonder."

"Out with it, Whiskers," Lord Benson said quietly.

"Perhaps you'll say I've got religion," the ex-officer said, "but it isn't that. I think it's because I've had lots and lots of time to think. Now I know that both of you understand far more about the universe than I ever could. But I'm quite sure that you would be the first to admit you know but a tiny fraction."

Sir Billy and Lord Benson silently nodded their heads in agreement.

"Very well," Whiskers plunged on. "The universe is older and more complicated than the human mind can conceive. It's older than we can imagine, even if we accept the big-bang theory of its creation, for there must have been something in existence long before that. It's larger, for we can't—at least I can't—visualize infinity, and that is its size. It's more complicated because there exists infinite variety ranging from the component parts of electrons to the vast galaxies that litter the universe. Yet everything is so well ordered. So, as I see it, the human mind is not the greatest thing in all the universe."

"Then what is?" Lord Benson asked quietly. He'd never heard Whiskers talk like this before.

The ex-officer flushed a brilliant red.

"I think there must be a God," he blurted out.

His friends could see how difficult it had been for him to

say this. They had never heard him mention religion. It was something one didn't talk about. Now here he was confessing a belief!

Like Whiskers, Lord Benson and Sir Billy had avoided thinking out their beliefs in the past. As scientists they both appreciated the infinite wonder of the universe and never ceased to marvel at its intricate and beautiful arrangement. But only in fleeting moments had they allowed themselves to speculate whether anything lay behind it, whether there was any reason for it and any direction in which it was moving.

"What's all this leading up to?" Billy asked. He didn't want to be pressed on his own beliefs. If he was, then he wouldn't know what to answer.

Whiskers had got over the worst. He'd made his declaration of faith, and his two friends hadn't ridiculed him.

"Well, if there is a God, surely we haven't any need to fear the alien," he said. "It's obvious that this visitor is far more technically advanced than we are. The inference is that he comes from a race that has been developing far longer than ours has. Developing and evolving. Surely, if you admit to the existence of a Supreme Being, an Infinite Intelligence, this development and evolution must be good. Unless, of course, you believe that God Himself is evil."

"What you are saying," Lord Benson interposed, "is that because this Vari must come from an older race, it must necessarily be from a more advanced and intelligent race. That evolution is always toward a higher plane, is always an advance."

"Something like that," Whiskers agreed. He was silently collecting his thoughts for a few seconds before he went on.

"Evolution has a definite direction and objective," he declared firmly. "I believe it is toward God Himself."

107

"That's a pretty staggering thing to say, "Billy Gillanders observed. "I couldn't go along with you that far. Oh, I agree that on Earth evolution has moved steadily from the single-celled amoeba to the human thinking brain. But many other things have evolved, too. Animals, viruses, reptiles, fungi, plants, microbes."

"Oh, I know that," Whiskers persisted, "but the general direction has always been upward. Though there have been setbacks and sidetracks, the trend has been toward greater intelligence. In another hundred thousand years —a million years—our descendants will be far more intelligent and have far greater mental powers than we have."

"More like God, in fact?" Billy asked quietly.

"Precisely. Though I can't conceive of any race being His equal, I believe that they will be much nearer than we are."

"So what you are saying is that because this alien comes from a far more technically advanced civilization than ours, from a race that must have been evolving far longer than ours, they must be nearer and more like God than we are?" Lord Benson inquired.

"That is my belief," Whiskers answered simply.

Neither of his two friends knew quite what to say. The three looked at each other uncomfortably for at least half a minute.

"So you say Chris has no need to fear this Vari? That he must be good and intend no harm?" Billy burst out.

"I do," agreed Whiskers.

"I pray you are right," Lord Benson muttered fervently.

13

"WALK," Vari had said.

With Colin close behind him, Chris stepped one pace forward. It was impossible, of course. How could one solid pass through another? Well, here goes, he thought.

He took a second step forward, and then another.

He couldn't believe it! That last stride should have taken him bang up against the side of the strange spaceship. He should have felt the hard, firm outer surface. He didn't. He walked *through* it!

He knew he was through and inside the spaceship, for the light was different. Instead of the harsh glare of Ariel's landscape, with its double shadows from Uranus and the Sun, Chris was suddenly surrounded by a soft, golden light. While his mind was still numbed, his eyes were questing around.

This couldn't be a spaceship! There was none of the massive array of instruments, dials, controls, screens, and lights that he'd always been used to. Instead he seemed to have stepped into a fairly spacious room, peculiar in shape, but an ordinary room nevertheless.

The golden light filled the whole chamber and Chris's eyes sought its source, but in vain. It was impossible to say that the light was coming from one place any more than from another. But it was certainly very restful after the brilliant illumination outside.

Suddenly he was aware that Colin was standing at his side. From his very attitude the leader could tell that his fellow astronaut was no more able to understand the situation than he was himself. He stretched out his gloved hand to give his colleague a reassuring pat.

Then the most incredible thing happened. Chris's hand felt nothing solid! It went straight through Colin's space suit as if he hadn't been there!

Chris had a sudden sick feeling in his stomach. What had happened? Had he gone mad? His mind couldn't adjust itself to what his senses told him was happening. He pulled back his hand sharply, as if he'd been burned.

Was it a hallucination? It must be. To reassure himself, Chris gingerly put his hand on Colin's shoulder.

He touched nothing! Again his hand felt no resistance from the space suit. Neither he nor Colin was solid!

Through his visor Chris could see the stupefied expression on his companion's face, for Colin must have seen what had happened. Their radios were not working, so neither could speak to the other.

"You are welcome," the voice of Vari suddenly said.

The voice still sounded very friendly. Chris looked to see where it was coming from but saw nothing. Why could Vari speak to them over their helmet radios, and yet they were unable to speak to each other? This was but one of the flood of questions that was making Chris's mind reel.

The alien must have been aware of the mental distress of the two astronauts.

"I am going to return your atoms to their former state," he said "You will then become what you call solid again. If you care to, you can remove your helmets, for I breathe almost the same atmosphere that you do."

"Where—are you?" Chris managed to croak. Could Vari hear him, or was the radio working one way only?

"You will see me in good time," the friendly voice answered. "I must give you time for your minds to accept the things you have seen so far."

They had certainly had enough fantastic experiences to be going on with, Chris agreed mentally. But he'd like to meet the alien face to face.

Both astronauts were aware of the same tingling sensation that they had felt when outside the ship, but it was gone in less than a minute. Experimentally, Chris put out his hand to touch his friend. This time Colin's shoulder was solid enough. In one of those strange spontaneous gestures that men sometimes make when under extreme stress, the two clasped each other's hands tightly. They needed to feel the firm pressure of a companion.

The moment of emotion was soon over, and their natural courage asserted itself. Now the question was, Should they remove their space helmets? Wearing them, they were at least sure of being able to breathe, even though they could only communicate with each other with gestures. Could they trust Vari? Was the atmosphere of the alien spaceship breathable or did it consist of poisonous gases that would burn up their lungs?

Again the decision was left to Chris. He could see Colin looking at him for a lead.

The choice wasn't really very hard to make. So far Vari hadn't deceived them. Even when he'd made the incredible statement that they would be able to walk through the shell of his ship, he had been right. This being from another world had them completely at his mercy. If he wished he could hold them prisoners within his vessel. But he'd shown no sign of hostility, and, on the contrary, seemed anxious to make their acquaintance. If the atmosphere was poisonous, they would be dead in a few minutes. If they declined to remove their helmets, they could still die within the ship, but their going would be long and drawn out.

Chris signaled to Colin. They would take Vari at his word!

As he removed the last clips that secured his helmet, Chris drew a deep breath. If Vari had deceived them and the atmosphere in the ship was poisonous, it would be the last normal one he would ever take. Perhaps the next would be of searing gases that would scorch his lungs or kill him instantly. With his pulse beating more quickly than usual, he whipped off his last protection from this strange world.

He didn't try to hold his breath any longer. He blew out atmosphere that had come all the way from Earth and refilled his lungs!

The air was cool and pleasant, perhaps with a slight scent. Chris took several deep breaths—and found them good. A feeling of exhilaration began to creep over him. It was great to be free from the restrictions of the space helmet!

"Whew! That's better!"

Colin, too, had removed his headgear and was drinking in long drafts of the delightful air. It was good, too, to be able to speak to each other.

"Where is he?" Colin asked.

"My friends, are you prepared to see me?"

Vari's voice, like the light, came from no definable direction. He might have been standing in the same room—but he was not.

"We are ready," Chris replied firmly. Had they not come all the way from Earth for this very purpose? He was sure they could now face meeting Vari himself.

"Very well!" the friendly voice answered. "So that you will not be too much surprised, I must tell you that my atoms are permanently arranged so that I can pass through what you call solids. I am in a small compartment alongside the room in which you are standing. I am going to appear before you—now!"

Neither Chris nor Colin was looking in exactly the right place at the time, for they had no indication where the small compartment was. Suddenly they both saw, out of the corner of their eyes, someone standing in the room. Vari had appeared!

Colin had been fearing this encounter more than Chris. Though Vari had said that he'd been sent to make contact with Earth people because he was very much like them, Colin had expected the worst. He'd pictured Vari as, perhaps, a two-headed monster or maybe a giant snake.

Instead the creature they saw before them was a handsome human being!

Vari seemed tall—nearly seven feet, Chris guessed. He had an open, smiling face with well-made features. His hair, blond, was a mass of tight curls. He wore a shining white tunic, and round the waist he had a broad belt on which were fastened what Chris guessed were small pieces of equipment. His feet were encased in what appeared to be soft leather boots.

Vari remained silent and smiling as his visitors got over their first shock. Somehow Colin found their host vaguely familiar, though he couldn't think why.

"Hello!" Chris said.

Afterward, when he remembered this moment, he blushed with shame. This was the only word he could think of on that tremendous occasion.

"Greetings—and welcome!" the alien returned. "Please relax and be at ease."

"Why—you're like us!" Colin burst out.

"I told you that." Vari smiled. "And may I repeat—you need have no fear."

"Where do you come from? Why are you here?" Chris now managed to ask.

"I come from a distant world in this galaxy," Vari replied in his pleasant voice. "Distant, that is, in your terms. But in universal terms we are near neighbors. I come to find out if your people are yet ready to meet us. We have no desire to come until you are."

"What do you mean by being ready?" Chris asked.

"Meeting me has been a terrific experience for you," Vari explained. "Yet you are young men, trained and conditioned to the highest point of your civilization. How much more terrifying would I be to the ordinary people of your world? We have no intention of thrusting ourselves upon you until your people are ready to meet us in friendship and goodwill."

"So we are here for you to find out?"

"Yes, my friends, you are," Vari smiled. "The whole operation has been carefully planned. We have watched your technical progress with interest. You have now reached the point when members of your race—yourselves—can meet us far away from your Earth. We have had to wait until now for this kind of meeting to take place."

"So you are using us as 'specimens'?" demanded Colin.

"In a way, yes. But please do not be angry. I hope you will find the experience as happy and pleasant as I shall."

"What do you mean by 'this kind of meeting'?" Chris asked. "Is there any other kind you have planned?"

"We have been visiting your Earth and meeting your people for centuries," Vari answered, "but I will tell you about that later. We believe that the time has now come for this contact to be known by all."

"But if you think Earthmen are ready to meet you, why don't you come and visit us?" Chris persisted.

"Because if we're wrong, a landing on your world by me or my fellows could cause universal panic. We couldn't take the risk as yet. So we had to extract a sample—you—to make sure you are ready. You see," Vari went on, "we would come in peace. But if your people became badly scared as our spaceships approached, then you would take hostile action, and perhaps put back our encounter for a century."

"So you want us to tell our people that you are all right and that we should hang out banners when you come," Colin suggested.

"You have a quaint way of putting it," Vari agreed, "but basically you are right. As I have already told you, we beamed those signals at you so that someone would come here and investigate. We had to make the signals slightly uncomfortable, but they would have done you no permanent harm."

"Now we're here, what do you want us to do?" Chris asked.

"I would like to exchange ideas with you and your companions, to ask and answer many questions, for you to find out much about me and my people, and for me to learn about you and your people," Vari said seriously. "Then we can decide if our spaceships are to visit your Earth."

"But if you have been monitoring our broadcasts for many years, you must know all about us," Colin pointed out.

"We do know a great deal. Your languages, much of your history, a good idea of your technology. But we have no up-to-date assessment of your spiritual development," explained Vari. "To us this is as important as all the rest put together. It is on this that we shall decide whether or not our contact can be expanded and made permanent. Or whether we have to be patient for a few more centuries."

"You keep saying 'we,'" Chris interposed. "What is your setup? How is your world directed and controlled?"

"That's difficult to answer shortly." The alien smiled. "Briefly, my world—and yours—is but one among millions of planets on which life is developing. These worlds are at all stages of development. Yours is a very young world. My own is a little older. Some are very much older.

"On them life has developed to a degree which you cannot imagine and which I also find difficult to picture.

At the apex of all this, somewhere, is what one can call the Supreme Intelligence directing and guiding your world, my world, and countless others, too."

"That's—that's God! gasped Colin.

"Then there is a Deity?" Chris burst out.

"Call the Supreme Intelligence what you will," Vari replied, "but it certainly exists. How could it be otherwise? You have seen the progress made by life on your Earth in a mere two and a half thousand million years. You have had intelligent, thinking life for only about half a million years. My world has had it for twice that time, and others many times more. All are evolving toward the ultimate—toward the Supreme Intelligence. Otherwise, why should life evolve at all?"

Chris and Colin were silent. Neither could find anything to say.

14

"Gosh! Did you see that?" Norman Spier spluttered to Morrey.

The two astronauts, following Chris's instructions, had remained in Alpha, but were, of course, glued to the observation window. They had seen Chris and Colin outside the alien spaceship. They had heard their conversation with Vari and had listened incredulously to the alien's statement that their friends would be able to walk through the ship's solid wall. Then, quite suddenly, Chris and Colin had disappeared. They had passed through the outer wall into the ship!

"It isn't possible!" Morrey breathed. "Yet it must have happened. Hey, Chris! Are you all right?"

There was a stony silence. They tried again to call their friends on the radio. But not a syllable did they get in return.

"What's happened to them?" gasped Norman.

"I don't know," Morrey snapped, a sure sign that he was desperately worried.

"They shouldn't have gone near," Norman blurted out. "He's got them."

"Stop that! It won't help."

"What can we do? Shall we go and have a look?"

"The first thing we must do is to report this. Give me the microphone. I'll let Beta know."

They hadn't been getting signals from Earth for some

time. Was it any use trying to let Sir Billy know what had happened? Even if the information reached him, there was nothing he could do. Anyway, they would let their friends in Beta know all about it.

As soon as Beta appeared over the horizon, Morrey told the crew what had happened—that Chris and Colin had apparently vanished into the alien ship and that their radios were silent. Serge and his crew were equally worried, and the Russian suggested that he should land his ship alongside Alpha so that they could act together.

"No," Morrey replied thoughtfully. "Stay where you are. If necessary, you can blast off back to Earth. There's no need for you to be trapped too. Are you getting Control?"

Serge replied that they were not. Nor could they pick up anything from elsewhere. It seemed that all they could receive was their sister ship. And they were thankful for that.

The two crews discussed at length the disappearance of Chris and Colin. In spite of the assurances of Morrey and Norman, the Beta astronauts still found it almost impossible to believe that their two colleagues had simply walked into the alien ship through the solid casing—and had vanished.

"What are we going to do?" the anguished voice of Tony sounded over the radio. "We can't just leave them there."

"Let me have a go and see if I can blast a way in with a laser gun," suggested Norman, but both Morrey and Serge were firmly against such action at this stage.

"I think we'll have to be patient for an hour or two," Morrey decided. "Then I'll get forward and have a snoop on my own."

Neither he nor any of the other five astronauts ever thought of blasting off and leaving Chris and Colin to their fate.

118

"Even if it's against orders, I'm not going to leave here until I've had a blast at that monstrosity," Norman promised himself. He looked meaningfully across at the rack where the laser guns were kept.

Meanwhile, Morrey was keeping up a constant radio call for Chris or Colin. Every half minute or so he would speak their names and request them to answer. The radio was silent except for the occasional interruption from the Beta crew.

As time passed, both Morrey and Norman began to wonder if they had really seen Chris and Colin vanish through the wall of the spaceship. Had their two colleagues simply walked round the far side of the alien ship so that they were now out of sight? Yet if that was so, they could still answer the urgent calls from their worried friends. Unless, of course, they had both met with an accident and were unable to reply.

Morrey felt he must settle his doubt once and for all. "I'm going to have a walk round that ship," he announced suddenly.

"Let me go," Norman pleaded. "You're better here in charge of communications."

"No, you had a nasty bash on that head of yours. Help me on with the suit," Morrey ordered.

Norman, disappointed, obliged, and soon the American was ready for his excursion. Beta had moved beyond radio range, so Norman wondered if it wouldn't be best to wait until their sister ship had reappeared.

"No," said Morrey, "it's no use wasting time."

In reality he wanted to avoid any argument with Serge and his crew. Though he was second in command to Chris, Morrey knew that Serge, his next in seniority, would strongly oppose this venture. So by the time Beta completed its next circuit, Morrey wanted his excursion to be an accomplished fact. With Norman's somewhat reluctant help, he put on his space suit and helmet and went through the airlock.

This was Morrey's first step onto the hostile surface of Ariel, and like the others he found it reminded him very much of the Moon. But there was one great difference between the satellites of Earth and Uranus, for here lurked the strange spaceship that seemed to have swallowed up his two friends.

Resolutely but carefully, Morrey began to walk to the alien vessel. All the time he kept up a running commentary over his radio to Norman back in Alpha. This was more to let him know that all was well than for any specific purpose. He knew that if Norman failed to hear his voice, he'd be into his own suit and out of their ship in a trice.

By earthly standards the alien ship looked enormous. Its lack of aerodynamic shape was puzzling, unless, of course, it never had to move in an atmosphere. Now that he was getting nearer, Morrey was looking at the monster vessel closely in a vain attempt to discover any break in the seemingly smooth and solid casing. If he could believe his eyes—if it wasn't, indeed, a hallucination—it was just about here that Chris and Colin had vanished. He redoubled his caution.

Perhaps, after all, it wouldn't have been a bad idea to have brought along a laser gun. What its effect might be on the ship or on Vari himself, Morrey had no idea. But it would, at least, have given him some feeling of protection. As it was, he had the creepy sensation that the alien was narrowly watching his steady advance.

When he came to within thirty yards of the ship, Morrey began to circle it. In spite of a close scrutiny, he could detect no opening. He paused for several minutes opposite the spot where Chris and Colin had disappeared, but there was nothing different here from any other part of the spaceship. Then he moved on.

Though he really didn't believe the possibility, he scanned the landscape to see if, by any chance, the two astronauts were on the far side of the ship. Of course they were not, and as Morrey trudged on to complete his circuit, he had to admit that the only place in which his two friends could be was inside the spaceship itself.

A wave of alarm and anger flooded over him—alarm for the safety of Chris and Colin and anger at the monstrosity squatting on the satellite's surface like a huge, shapeless jellyfish. And this creature or thing had swallowed up two young men!

"Not a sign of them," he reported over his radio. "I'm going closer."

"Be careful," came the agonized voice of Norman, "and don't do any disappearing tricks. I've no fancy for being left alone."

"And I don't want to be swallowed up," Morrey replied shortly.

Slowly he walked toward the alien ship. Now that he had convinced himself that his two friends had disappeared inside—not that he really needed convincing—Morrey approached the sinister shape with extreme caution. After every step he paused for a few seconds to look around sharply.

Nothing happened, and at last he was right up to the ship's side. This would be approximately where Chris and Colin had stepped through, and Morrey, his pulse beating a little faster, stopped.

It looked, even from here, absolutely solid. He put his hand out very carefully toward the casing. An inch away, he hesitated. Would it burn him or electrocute him? Well, his gloves should provide insulation so—here goes.

He touched the outer casing. Nothing happened. Apart from its unusual texture, the ship's wall looked and felt perfectly normal. It was solid enough beneath the pressure of his hand. Morrey was tempted to thump hard on the surface—perhaps to get through to his missing friends—but long training had conditioned him against doing anything that might damage his protective clothing. So he was about to turn away in disgust when he saw at his feet a nice, rounded piece of rock.

Just the thing to throw at the spaceship! Not that it would do it any harm. But at least it would be a gesture of his hostility to the thing that seemed to have engulfed his friends. He bent down and picked up the piece of rock. It fitted snugly into the palm of his gloved hand. Then he stepped a pace or two away and lobbed the rock like a baseball.

It would just bounce off, of course, and fall to the ground. But it didn't. It passed right through the casing and vanished from sight!

It fell with a clatter a few yards behind where Chris and Colin stood talking to Vari.

"Your friends are getting a little impatient, it seems," the alien observed. "Would you like to contact them?"

Chris looked surprised. He had been so much absorbed in the conversation with Vari that he thought only a few minutes had passed.

"How did the rock get inside?" Colin asked, bending down to pick up Morrey's missile.

"The outer casing of this ship is in a permanent state of atomic alignment," Vari explained. "That means that anything that is also in a similar state can pass through it. This rock, which must be from immediately alongside, would have been in a similar condition. Hence its atoms were able to pass through the ship's atoms."

"Can we walk through the wall again?" Colin asked.

"Not as you are," Vari told them. "I restored you to your former condition just after you entered. You seemed a little startled at being able to pass through each other's bodies, so I mixed up your atoms again so that you would not feel so strange. You see, for two objects to pass through each other, both have to be in a state of atomic alignment. If one of them is not, then the phenomenon cannot occur."

Chris looked very thoughtful.

"So the atmosphere in the ship isn't lined up? Otherwise it would all escape?" he asked.

"Precisely." Vari smiled. "Likewise the ground on which we are resting isn't aligned. If it were, we might sink to the center of the satellite."

"Hadn't we better get back to Alpha?" inquired Colin anxiously. "They will wonder what's happened to us."

"I suppose so." Chris sighed. He would have liked to spend many hours talking to Vari and absorbing the wonders of the new knowledge he brought.

"Perhaps you have had enough for one lesson," Vari said with a twinkle. "Maybe you can persuade your friends to come with you next time."

Chris didn't reply. He would have to sort out his own ideas first. Where would he begin to tell the others of all the wonders that he and Colin had seen?

"Are you ready?" Vari asked, and Chris nodded.

Vari merely touched one of the tiny pieces of equipment on his belt and immediately the astronauts felt the same tingling sensation as their atoms took up position.

"Off you go," Vari said, as the tingling died away, "and come back soon. I can pick up your radios, so you have only to say when you are ready. Good-bye, my friends."

Chris raised his hand in a gesture of farewell. He and Colin had replaced their helmets and were ready to step outside. Again they were to have that remarkable experience of walking through a wall. But they had done it once, and this time they didn't doubt that it could happen. At a sign from their host they strode forward—and found themselves outside the ship in the brilliant glare of the barren landscape.

Even as they paused to adjust themselves to their surroundings, a tumult broke out over their radios.

"Chris! Colin! Are you all right?"

"Where have you been? Have you seen Vari?"

"We tried to contact you, but we couldn't."

"What's happened?"

Morrey from twenty yards away and Norman from inside Alpha poured out their flood of questions. One moment the huge alien spaceship had been all that they could see. The next second Chris and Colin were standing alongside it. It seemed like magic.

"We're all right," Chris replied shortly. "Let's get back to the ship."

So much had happened in such a short time that his mind hadn't quite adjusted itself to the situation. He must return to the more familiar surroundings of Alpha's cabin so that he could take a grip on himself. No wonder Vari said that he and his kind had to be very careful about when to reveal themselves to humans.

Morrey and Norman sensed that their two friends had been through a tremendous experience and were struggling to adjust themselves to it. The three astronauts made their way silently back to the ship, and not a word was spoken until they were almost at the foot of Alpha's ladder. It was then that Colin stopped and suddenly exploded into speech.

"I know! I've got it," he burst out. "Vari looks like the picture of an archangel!"

15

THIS ONLY CONFIRMED Morrey's worst fears. He bundled the dazed Colin up the ladder and pushed him through the airlock first. Chris went next, for his mind was still totally preoccupied, and he let the American push him forward. Morrey breathed a sigh of relief when he had entered the cabin and was able to seal the airlock safely behind them.

"Help them," he snapped to Norman as soon as he'd taken off his own helmet. Chris, with a visible effort, jerked his thoughts back to his surroundings.

"It's all right," he said weakly. "We're not ill. Just— staggered."

Morrey insisted on all space suits being removed and stowed away before he would let either Chris or Colin speak. Meanwhile, he was eyeing them closely.

"Now can we speak?" Chris asked with a patient smile as the four astronauts relaxed on their couches.

"What—what did Colin mean?" Norman stammered. "Is he okay?"

"I know what he means," Chris answered quickly, before Colin could find words. "We've met Vari face to face, and I must say that I understand Colin's reaction. We've all seen traditional pictures of archangels—Gabriel or Michael. Well, Vari looks like one of those, except that he hasn't got wings."

"Lucifer looked like that, too," Norman pointed out darkly.

Chris went on quickly. "We'll tell you all that happened. Our radio couldn't penetrate the electrical field round his ship, so we couldn't call you or receive you."

Then, frequently interrupted by Colin, Chris gave a detailed account of all that had happened and all that Vari had said to them after they had stepped into the alien spaceship. He described the moment when his hand passed through Colin's body and the queasy feeling it gave him. He repeated all that Vari had told them about the purpose and direction of life, and how Vari himself came from a race which was far more advanced along the evolutionary road than humans were.

He went on to explain that Vari—or those who sent him—had planned to get them to this outpost of the solar system so that an assessment could be made as to whether Earthmen were ready to meet Vari and his fellows openly. If not, then mankind would have to wait still longer for the inevitable contact to be made.

Both Morrey and Norman had listened silently to this astounding story. The crew of Beta had also listened over the radio. But now Morrey found his feelings sharply divided. Of course, he was filled with wonder at what he himself had seen and what Chris had told him. At the same time, he felt deep misgivings about the encounter and its possible consequences. It was likely, he thought, that his two friends had somehow been hypnotized by the alien. Certainly Colin had if he thought Vari looked like a wingless angel.

While Morrey had every admiration and respect for his leader's mental powers, he told himself that Chris had been up against something literally "out of this world." There was no knowing what hypnotic powers the alien might

126

possess as well as the extraordinary technical ability he had demonstrated. Perhaps it was all part of Vari's plan to ingratiate himself with the leader of the expedition.

"You must be hungry. Let's have a meal," Morrey suggested. This was really because he wished to give himself more time to think.

What would be the position if Chris's intellect had been undermined by his contact with Vari? Was he still capable of making a rational decision, or would he now be just the alien's instrument? It would be a terrible thing if he, Morrey, had to take over command because of the incapacity of his leader.

He couldn't ask Beta's crew what they thought about it all, for he would have to speak in front of Chris himself. It would be easier if Beta landed, and he could consult Serge and the others.

As they were relaxing and eating their meal, Morrey suggested that now there seemed no danger from the alien, it would be a good idea to call Beta down rather than leave the crew to circle monotonously overhead.

"Oh, yes, let's come and join in the fun," Tony's voice said.

"Very well," Chris agreed. "Come in on your next orbit, Beta." He'd no idea what Morrey's real motive had been in proposing the landing, but he thought it would be as well for him and Colin to brief all the astronauts thoroughly before their next encounter with Vari. The alien himself wanted to meet all the Earthmen; perhaps he could arrange for all of them to visit his ship. Then Morrey and the rest could see this wonderful being for themselves.

Morrey was talking to Beta over the radio and indicating where he thought a suitable nearby landing place would be. He was secretly relieved that Chris had so easily accepted his suggestion to call in Beta. If the leader had still insisted on their sister spaceship continuing her lonely vigil, then Morrey would have been faced with his terrible decision much sooner than he'd hoped.

As they waited for Beta to complete its orbit, the Alpha crew continued to talk about their contact with Vari.

"Why is he blocking our radio communication with the Cape?" Morrey demanded. "That isn't a very friendly act, is it?"

For some reason Chris felt slightly irritated at his friend's question.

"I hope you'll soon be able to ask him that yourself. I expect he doesn't want us to give Control our first impressions of him," he replied defensively.

"But why not?" Norman wanted to know. "We should have given a factual report."

"Yes, but we know so few of the facts at the moment," Chris pointed out. "My guess is that when we've had time to find out more and to make a balanced judgment, he'll take away the radio block."

"I hope you're right," Morrey muttered. "Do you trust him, Chris?"

The leader thought carefully. What really was his impression, so far, of Vari? And could that impression be relied upon? He looked handsome and trustworthy, angelic, in fact. But Norman had pointed out that Lucifer, the wicked angel, had also been handsome. Was Vari's appearance deceptive too?

"I think I do," Chris replied to Morrey's question. "What else can we do?"

It was indeed a critical question. The alien certainly had the technical ability to make their escape impossible. Would he use that ability? If, as Chris thought, he wouldn't, they would be able to get away. But then Vari would rightly conclude that the human race was still so obsessed with distrust and hostility that contact must be still further delayed.

On the other hand, if Vari were to hold his visitors prisoner, then all Chris's ideas would be proved wrong. The alien's angelic appearance would be deceptive and that high-minded talk about all evolution being directed by and toward the Supreme Intelligence would be a gigantic lie. The scheme of things as outlined by the alien was so attractive and exciting, made life so worthwhile and logical, that if it wasn't true, Chris didn't want to know. If life was just a chance development amid universal chaos, it seemed a waste. If it had no purpose or objective, then all the highest incentives to progress were just self-deception. How flat everything would now seem if all that Vari had said was untrue.

"I must trust him," Chris muttered to himself. "If I can't, life is no longer worthwhile."

Colin had been answering the hundred and one questions that had been fired at him by the envious Norman. From the few replies that Chris listened to, the leader could tell that his companion was equally impressed by the alien.

"He really is a fine big man," Colin was assuring Norman, "that is—if you can say he's a man. He was friendly and smiled often. I think he's anxious to handle us gently and to make a good impression on us. You'll like him."

Both Chris and Morrey heard Colin's last remark. It pleased Chris; it alarmed Morrey. Obviously the sooner the rest of us meet Vari, the better, Chris thought. But Morrey had no wish for himself or the other crew members to fall under the hypnotic influence of the alien. Yet he didn't see how he could avoid it unless he revolted against Chris's leadership. It might come to that—but not yet.

Beta made a perfect landing about six hundred yards

129

from her sister ship. Morrey and Norman were nominated to go out and welcome the Beta crew, and they were already waiting for their friends to emerge some time before the ground was cool enough. At last, when the regulation time had elapsed, the airlock opened, and Robert Campbell came clambering down the steps.

There was an excited exchange of banter over the radios as Tony, Mervyn Williams, and Serge followed and made their way to Alpha. After so long cooped up in a cabin it felt good to have the freedom of the open, and the newly arrived astronauts displayed their exhilaration by disporting themselves under the low gravity of Ariel. They would leap many feet into space and then fall back as if in a slow-motion film. They would take prodigious strides forward or jump along like a kangaroo.

It was while this horseplay was going on that Morrey tried to attract Serge's attention. Serge looked at him curiously and was about to ask what was wrong when he saw, through the visor, the worried look on Morrey's face. He flashed a question with his eyes, but Morrey was unable to explain.

It was in a rather crowded cabin that the eight astronauts met. The facade of jokes and banter failed to conceal their joy and relief at being together once more. Perhaps, united, they could face the challenge of Vari's presence with calm.

After a time Morrey was able to detach Serge from the rest. By a significant glance he invited the Russian to follow him up into the "fridge," the hypothermia compartment. There they could talk for a little while without being overheard.

"Serge," Morrey began quickly. "I'm worried about Chris. He seems to be obsessed by this alien. And Colin thinks Vari looks like an archangel. I think they're both under his influence—hypnotized, perhaps. He wants us all to go and meet the creature. What do you advise?"

130

"Well, we came all this way for that purpose," Serge pointed out. "Is there any reason why we shouldn't?"

"And all be hypnotized? It's too big a risk, Serge. I feel some of us, at least, should keep our distance. I'm not convinced he's friendly."

"But he's not shown any sign of unfriendliness, has he?"

"Not yet. He's too clever. I think we should get away. Let's report to Control all we've found out so far. Thanks to Vari's 'friendliness,' we can't use the radio. Chris even finds excuses for him for that!"

"Did Chris and Colin really walk through the solid wall?"

"That's what it seemed to us," Morey replied. "But what I wanted to ask you was—if Chris tells us all to go into the alien's spaceship, what do we do?"

"Go in, of course," Serge replied promptly. "You haven't any other suggestion, have you?"

Morrey was most uncomfortable. Chris had been his great friend and leader for a long time. They had faced innumerable perils together. They were bound together by invisible bonds. So what should he do if he conscientiously thought that Chris's judgment had been impaired? Wasn't it his duty to disobey any order arising from that faulty judgment?

"But suppose the alien has hypnotized him," he replied to Serge. "Don't you think we ought to keep out of his clutches?"

"We have no evidence that Chris or Colin has been hypnotized. Until we have, then, we do what he says," Serge said firmly.

Morrey was more uncertain than ever. He'd expected at least moral support from his next senior colleague. But he was determined that he himself wouldn't fall under the alien's spell.

"We'd better rejoin the others," Serge advised.

"Okay, but watch out," Morrey agreed grudgingly.

It was plain that before long the astronauts would have to pay a second visit to the alien from another world, but because of the strain and excitement to which they had all been subject, Chris very wisely decided to postpone the visit until they had all had a rest period. So after two hours in Alpha's crowded cabin, he ordered the Beta quartet to return to their ship. They would all set out to meet Vari in twelve hours' time.

Both Chris and Colin wished for nothing better than to extend their contact with the handsome, smiling visitor. Morrey was definitely against it and was determined to avoid the visit at all costs. Norman had been infected by Morrey's doubts and so, to tell the truth, had Serge. But Tony, Robert, and Mervyn could hardly wait for the meeting.

Few of the astronauts slept well. They were looking forward to the visit to the alien ship with either excitement or apprehension, and long before the twelve hours were over, they were all up and about. Tony was far too excited to eat, a most unusual state for him.

"Hello, Vari," Chris called over the radio. "Are you getting me? May we come over?"

"Greetings, my friends," the reply came instantly. "You are all welcome. Call me when you are outside my ship so that I can let you enter. I am sorry some of you haven't slept well."

"How the blazes did he know that?" Morrey asked, but no one seemed to hear him in the bustle of putting on space suits.

"Er—Chris," Morrey said a moment later, "don't you think it would be advisable for someone to remain behind in each ship? I suppose we could get a stray meteorite."

Chris paused in his task. He hadn't suggested this rather unnecessary precaution because he thought all the astronauts would be so eager to meet Vari. Still, if someone volunteered, that would be a different matter. So Morrey and Serge agreed to remain in their ships while the others went forward. Poor Norman was going with great misgivings, but he could think of no excuse for dropping out.

"Ready?" Chris called over the radio.

The six astronauts had congregated at the foot of Alpha. Morrey and Serge were watching from the portholes of their respective ships. The great gamble was about to begin.

"Ready," the chorus went back to Chris, and they all set off.

Morrey watched with a heavy heart. This might be the last he would ever see of his friends. He prayed that he was wrong, but, somehow, he didn't think he was. Vari was too good to be true. There was a catch in it somewhere. In a moment of near panic he thought of imploring his friends to come back, but he remained silent as he watched them go.

16

Because all communication with the Uranus expedition had failed, there was an air of gloom at Cape Kennedy. Were Chris and his colleagues still alive? Had the creature from another world harmed them?

The director's anxieties and doubts were infectious, and Lord Benson was filled with despair. What could be done to help the astronauts? What could be done to find out if they were still alive? Nothing!

These feelings were widespread among the hundreds of scientists and technicians at the Cape. A suitably worded, but noncommittal, communiqué was issued to the world press. It didn't, of course, mention the existence of the alien, but most people believed that some great disaster had overwhelmed and obliterated the expedition—men and machines.

Only Whiskers refused to despair, though he had only his new faith in the existence of a Supreme Intelligence to support him. In the past he had been called upon many times to sustain the morale of the astronauts. Now, it seemed, an even greater task awaited him. How could he persuade Benny and Billy not to despair? He guessed that it would be little use to suggest that they all go to one of the churches or chapels at the Cape and pray. All he could do was to exude confidence in his faith and remain cheerful. He knew he would be proved right in the end.

Alone in Alpha, Morrey made a desperate resolve. If his friends were trapped in the alien spaceship, if they came to any harm, he would lift Alpha to a great height from Ariel, and then bring it crashing down onto the ugly monster. He would gladly give his own life to wreak revenge on the alien and—who knows?—perhaps stop him doing harm to others. So, with his mind made up, with a face as hard as granite, Morrey riveted his gaze on his six friends.

As he led his men forward, Chris was conscious that he headed a deputation of humans to a being from another world. Having met and talked to Vari, he was anxious that his companions should share his and Colin's experience. A pity that Serge and Morrey had had to be left behind.

But had they? The suggestion had come from Morrey, and though Chris had thought the precaution unnecessary, he'd agreed. Could it be that his two friends weren't anxious to meet Vari?

"Strange," he murmured to himself, "I wonder what's the matter with them."

By now the six astronauts had reached the side of the big spaceship.

"We're here, Vari," Chris called out, and immediately the reply came back.

"Please wait while I align your atoms."

The astronauts felt the slight tingling sensation that Colin and Chris had described. It soon passed, and Vari announced that they could now enter.

Without hesitation Chris stepped forward, followed by the other five. The next moment they were standing in a little group inside the ship, awaiting the appearance of their host.

"Hey! You're standing partly inside me!" the startled voice of Mervyn Williams burst out.

Chris turned and saw the incredible sight of Mervyn

and Robert partly intermingled with each other! Hastily they stepped apart, and then all six broke into rather nervous laughter.

"You get used to that kind of thing," said the voice of Vari, and they could detect amusement in his tones. "Won't you take off your helmets and be comfortable?"

The six were only too pleased to remove their headgear and take deep breaths of the ship's pleasant atmosphere. While they were chatting excitedly, Vari suddenly appeared. Again no one saw exactly where he came from, but the astronauts fell silent. Four of them were gazing for the first time on this being of an older race.

They could see at once what Colin had meant when he'd said that Vari reminded him of an archangel. Certainly the alien's tall and handsome figure brought back memories of pictures they had seen in childhood.

"You are all welcome," Vari began, "but why are you not all here?"

"We left two of our friends behind to keep an eye on our ships," Chris answered rapidly. He was very conscious of the weakness of this excuse.

"I see," Vari replied slowly, "but what would harm your ships if all your crews were here?"

Chris thought furiously. He didn't want to upset the alien, for plainly Vari was disappointed that Morrey and Serge had been left behind.

"Oh, just the odd meteorite might cause trouble. Our ships are not made like yours."

"I could have helped you," Vari told them. Did Chris detect a trace of reproach in the alien's voice?

"We've all come to hear more about your world and to let you learn more about ours," Chris said hurriedly. He wanted to divert the conversation away from the absent Morrey and Serge.

"We know a great deal about you already." Vari smiled.

136

"As I have told you, we monitor your radio and television. Before that, we sent our people to visit your Earth from time to time."

"You've been to Earth?" Tony asked. "How can that be?"

"We have sent our emissaries to live among you. They have been as you are and have lived as you do. Of course, your people did not realize that we were from another world. Usually they thought we were prophets and teachers of your own world."

"But how did you get there? In spaceships like this? How is it we never heard about it?" Robert demanded.

"Yes, we came in spaceships," Vari told him. "Always we tried to land on a deserted part of your planet so that we should not alarm you. And to prevent your knowing that we were among you, for that would have defeated our purpose."

"And what was your purpose?" asked Norman.

"We had, and still have, two main reasons for making contact with you." Vari said, smiling. "One is to find out how far you have progressed. The other is to give you just a little nudge along in the right direction."

"How do we know which is the right direction?" Norman persisted. "How do we know that yours is the right one?"

"Because it leads toward the Supreme Intelligence."

"But suppose we didn't want to go that way?"

"You would soon destroy yourselves," their host told Norman. "Alas, some races have done this, and we have no wish for humans to do the same."

"We have a choice?"

"Ultimately—no. Immediately—yes. Your present civilization may pursue a course that will end in self-destruction. It would be succeeded, sometime, by another civilization. That, too would have a choice. But only if it moved toward the Supreme Intelligence would a repetition of the process be avoided."

"How long has this been going on?" Tony asked.

"For ever," Vari told them, "and it will go on for ever. There is no beginning and no end."

"But I thought, according to the big-bang theory, that everything was created four and a half thousand million years ago," Tony protested.

"And what did your theorists think existed before their big bang? Time and matter certainly did. Why not another universe?"

Tony faded into silence. This was too much for him. Chris might understand what Vari was saying, but he certainly didn't. All he could make of it was that this person from a far distant world came from a much older and more advanced civilization than that on Earth, and that he or his fellows had visited Earth over the centuries. Maybe the ancients had seen them and thought they were angels. That would explain why Vari seemed familiar.

While his friends were asking innumerable questions, Tony let his own thoughts wander. It was staggering to learn that there were innumerable civilizations in the universe and that they were all at different stages of development. He supposed that humans were only in the very early stage and that Vari had come as a kind of missionary.

Tony remembered a book he'd once read about flying saucers and the controversy that surrounded reports of them. One section of the book had listed accounts of strange objects in the sky described in a wide variety of ancient writings. Even the Bible has passages that could refer to spaceships.

Now Tony could understand the origin of the classical stories about the gods. He remembered the legends of the Greeks, Romans, and Norsemen. He was more vague about those of other countries, but he had no doubt that all were founded, somehow, on people from other worlds like Vari. Then his attention was jerked back to the present.

"Would you like to inspect my ship?" Vari was asking.

There was a chorus of enthusiastic affirmatives, so with a graceful gesture Vari invited the company to follow him.

It still astounded his visitors to see Vari simply vanish through the solid wall of the compartment into another one. Led by Chris, the astronauts followed after only a momentary hesitation.

"This is where I sleep," Vari told the six, but the room, or cabin, seemed completely bare. Norman Spier was about to ask the question that was puzzling them all when Vari appeared to anticipate his inquiry.

"Of course, I don't use a bed as you do. I use a magnetic field. Watch," he said.

Again his hand touched that broad belt of his, and at once he appeared to float and hang, motionless, a few feet from the floor. There were no visible means of support.

"It's much more comfortable than your beds are, I expect," Vari said with a smile.

All the astronauts had done the same thing when they had been in a condition of free fall, or zero gravity, during their many spaceflights. But they never believed it to be possible when in a gravity field. Even though the attraction of Ariel, like that of the Moon, was small by earthly standards, it was sufficient to hold everything firmly to the ground. Vari's performance was certainly startling, but he soon stood back on his feet.

"Can we see your motors?" Tony asked. It would be interesting to see the ship's very advanced method of propulsion.

"Motors?" Vari was puzzled for a moment, and then he laughed.

"Why, of course," he agreed. "But you'll find things a bit strange. Come on."

139

17

Morrey had made up his mind.

More than anything he wanted to talk to Serge, but if he called him on the intership radio, the alien would be able to pick up their conversation. The only way he could speak to him in private was to make his way to Beta.

He couldn't even warn Serge that he was coming. This too, would be picked up by the alien, who would then know that remaining behind to watch over the ship's safety was only a subterfuge. If Serge suddenly saw his friend crossing from Alpha to Beta, would he call out and so give the show away? This was something that Morrey would have to risk.

He passed through the airlock and climbed down to the surface. It wouldn't be long, he guessed, before Serge would spot him. If he proceeded with caution and gave the impression of stealth, perhaps his friend would take the hint and remain silent.

With exaggerated caution, Morrey picked his way toward Beta. He almost held his breath as he waited for some exclamation to come from Serge over his helmet radio. But the seconds ticked by as he moved forward, and still no comment came from the Russian. Then he had an idea.

"I almost wish I'd gone with the others instead of being stuck here inside this cabin," he said into his radio.

There was scarcely a second's pause before the reply came from Serge.

"Yes, I'd rather be out there than in here," he said.

Good for Serge! He'd guessed that Morrey wanted his visit kept secret, so he'd played along with him. That could only mean that he shared some of Morrey's doubts about the alien. As he climbed Beta's ladder and entered the airlock, Morrey wondered whether he dared let his friend know of his desperate plan.

As soon as he entered Beta, he made sure that the radios were switched off, and asked Serge to help in keeping his visit secret. The Russian agreed readily, and throughout the time they were together they broke off periodically to talk over the radio as if they were back in their own ships.

"I'm quite sure he's hypnotized them," Morrey explained. "If he's as advanced in psychology as he is in physics, it would be child's play. I'm not going to let myself fall under his spell."

"It isn't certain," Serge pointed out. "Chris would not be deceived easily."

"I've the greatest affection and admiration for Chris," Morrey conceded, "But, after all, he's only one of us. He was as impressed as anyone when he walked through the alien ship's solid casing. No. I'm afraid Vari is miles ahead of us in every way. That would include manipulation of the mind."

"Are you saying that Vari has hypnotized our friends for some reason of his own?" Serge asked.

"I am—and I'm almost certain his reason is evil. Why has he cut off our communication with Control? Why can't we speak to our party in his ship? It can only mean that he doesn't want anyone to know what's happening in that ugly monster out there."

"Have you told Chris of your doubts?"

141

"What's the use? He seems completely taken in by this alien and is unlikely to listen to a word against him. If I'm right, it would be dangerous to say anything to Chris."

"Why?" Serge asked.

"Because he'd report it to Vari, and then Vari would know that you and I, at least, haven't been deceived. That could mean a pretty quick end for both of us."

"What do you suggest we do?"

"The most important thing is to avoid falling under the alien's influence ourselves. We must find every possible excuse for not coming into contact with him. Then we must persuade Chris to give the order to blast off. The sooner we are on our way home, the better. Maybe the alien's influence will wane after we start back to Earth."

"But suppose Chris refuses to order our return? What do you propose to do?"

This, of course, was the critical question. Morrey felt that he couldn't share his dreadful decision with his friend. No one else must know that he would use Alpha as a giant bomb in order to obliterate the alien and his influence.

"If Chris refuses to blast off, it will confirm my fears," he answered darkly. "I must then consider my position as second in command."

The implications of what the American had just said were too uncomfortable to contemplate. Yet Serge knew that if Chris became incapacitated either physically or mentally, it would be Morrey's duty to take over.

"I'd better return to Alpha," Morrey said after a long pause.

He plodded his way back while still keeping up the pretense, by his radio conversation with Serge, that he'd never left his ship. When he was safely inside Alpha's cabin, he removed his suit and stowed it away. Now he would try once more to contact the six in the alien's ship.

It was no use. Nor were any signals yet coming in from

Earth. Vari's barrage was still preventing communication with Control. Morrey fumed impotently. Oh, why couldn't Chris see that this alien was bent on their destruction? It was hard to keep up a carefree chat with Serge while every minute his misgivings increased. At last his self-control gave way.

"Curse you, Vari," he shouted into the microphone, "what have you done to my friends?"

Chris and his companions followed Vari across the cabin—they still thought of it as such, but it was more like a hall—and watched him fade through a certain part of the wall. With a humorous shrug of his shoulders, Chris followed.

The room they were in was very much smaller than the "hall." Again there was an almost complete lack of instruments; the only one that they could see was a panel of flickering lights that constantly changed color and pattern. However, this room had one prominent feature. It was a large, polished dome in the center of the floor.

Tony, who had followed Chris, halted.

"Where are your motors?" he asked.

"This is our 'motor,' " Vari replied, indicating the shining dome.

It was about ten feet high and about twenty feet in diameter. The outside seemed to be of some light-colored metal which reflected the images of the astronauts in grotesque shapes.

The humans looked at the alien incredulously. This was nothing like a motor as they understood it. Each of them had had experience of many kinds—chemical and atomic. But this was neither—if, indeed, it was a motor at all. Vari saw their bewilderment.

"We use a kind of energy that you know little about," he began.

"What is it?" Tony burst out, unable to restrain himself. "What energy do you use that we don't know about?"

"You do know something about it. Everyone in the universe does. It is what you call gravity."

"Gravity?" queried Norman. "How does that help you to cross space?"

"Just as you have discovered how to concentrate light in an intense beam, a laser, so my people can concentrate gravity. You can imagine how strong this can be if you think of the size of a planet like Uranus. Even this is minute compared with the vast suns that litter the universe. Gravity is the greatest source of power that exists—far beyond that provided by nuclear energy."

"Then what is this dome? How do you make use of these beams of gravity?" asked Chris.

"They crisscross the universe," Vari explained, "and this dome houses the apparatus that enables my ship to ride on any beam."

"How is it that we don't feel this gravity beam?"

"Because we change its nature at source. It requires a converter, such as this, to change it back. I'm afraid you would not understand how the gravity beam is changed, for it involves a branch of physics about which you as yet know nothing."

"So you can travel without carrying fuel with you?" persisted Tony. "This is all the engine you require?"

"The answer to both your questions is yes," Vari said, smiling. "The converter enables the ship to ride along any beam at a great speed, and the energy to do so is at the source. So, you see, I am not bothered with the masses of equipment that I understand are necessary for your ships."

So that was why all the rooms in Vari's ship seemed almost bare! That was why the vessel looked more like a strangely shaped house than a spaceship! This domed converter was capable of propelling the ship along the invisible gravity beams that crisscrossed space. What a wonderfully simple and economic way to travel.

"What speed do you reach?" Norman asked.

"How far have you come?" Colin inquired, almost at the same time.

"As I told you before, I come from a solar system in this same galaxy. My world is—to use your own unit of measurement—about seventy light years away, toward the central mass of the galaxy."

"So it's taken many years to get here?" asked the bewildered Tony.

"I was just about to tell you," the alien twinkled—"but you fire questions at me so rapidly. No, it didn't take very long. This ship is capable of a velocity many times greater than that of light. It took me about two of your weeks to come from my own world to your solar system."

"Two weeks!" several of the astronauts burst out together. "But that's impossible!"

"How can you travel faster than light?" Robert Campbell wanted to know.

"Oh, there are many things, you will find, that travel faster than light," Vari explained. "Already your physicists and mathematicians are talking about particles called tachyons which travel far faster than light. It is possible to break the light barrier, just as—many years ago—you were able to break the sound barrier. The velocity of gravity itself is almost instantaneous. You know that it is the pull of your Sun that holds your Earth to a circular path around it. If the Sun were to be destroyed, your Earth would shoot out into space immediately—not some eight minutes later, which is the time taken for the Sun's light to reach you."

It was too much. The six humans were overwhelmed with the glimpse Vari had given them of his technology.

So this was what man would be able to do in a thousand, perhaps ten thousand years' time. There was so much that the alien had told them that neither Chris nor his companions could ever begin to understand.

The idea that it would be possible to travel faster than light was contrary to all they had ever believed. Chris had heard vaguely of tachyons, but he'd thought these theoretical particles were merely the dreamstuff of abstract mathematicians. If what Vari had told them was correct, he thought with growing excitement, it would be possible to travel to distant reaches of the universe without the need for hypothermia.

The others, too, had begun to wonder about the outcome of this meeting. Perhaps they would return to Earth with information that could lead to a fantastic technological leap forward. Or maybe they would go back with just an incredible story. That Vari intended to harm them or that he wouldn't let them take off never occurred to them.

"Now may I have a turn asking the questions?" Vari said lightly. "Remember I want to find out about you just as much as you do about me."

"Sorry," Chris said, grinning, "but you have rather staggered us all. Ask what you like, and we'll try to answer."

Vari followed with a series of searching questions, not so much about the technical developments on Earth—about which he already seemed well informed—as about the people. What was their outlook, their attitude to each other, their moral and intellectual standards? Had they any idea about the direction in which the human race was moving? What was the strength of their belief in a God of some kind?

Chris and the others answered as best they could. Chris, at least, was very conscious of the importance of their answers. He guessed that Vari would decide from what they said whether or not contact with Earth could yet be made openly. It was to Vari's last question that he gave his most thoughtful reply.

"Do we believe in a God? Some do and some don't," Chris said. "Of course, beliefs in various kinds of gods were almost universal among our primitive races. Even those who had always been geographically isolated were found to have their beliefs in greater-than-human powers. Maybe your friends were responsible for this.

"In the more civilized parts of our planet, belief in God has fluctuated. Up until about a century ago, it was fairly general, but as we made important scientific discoveries, as we learned more about our Earth and the universe, as we thought we were wresting nature's secrets away from her, so belief in God began to crumble. Given time, man could know everything and would be all-powerful.

"Then things began to change once more. We realized that the universe, right from the ultimate particles of matter to the vast galaxies of unimaginable size, was infinitely more intricate than had been believed. For every new discovery that was made, complete understanding seemed to have slipped farther away. Gradually, I think, we are losing the arrogance that made us see man as the be-all and end-all of creation."

Vari listened in silence but said nothing. Suddenly Chris and the others felt tired. They had been inside the alien spaceship much longer than they realized, and the tremendous experience of meeting this being from another world was beginning to tell upon them. It was Chris, of course, who spoke for them all.

"I think we'd better return to our ships. We're still very shaken at meeting you, Vari," he said with a smile. "Don't think us rude if we go now. We'll come again soon—or perhaps you may care to visit us."

Even as Chris spoke, the astronauts sensed a change in the alien. Until now his handsome face had been smiling

147

and kind. Now, suddenly, it became serious—even stern.

A thousand thoughts flashed through Chris's mind. What was the reason for this change? Had they placed too much trust in Vari? Was Morrey right that the alien was trying to mislead them?

"What is it, Vari?" Chris asked. His throat went dry at the possibility of having their host as an enemy. There was an uneasy pause as the astronauts waited for him to speak.

18

"You do not represent all your race," the alien said coldly. "I have just had a hostile message from one of your friends."

"A hostile message?" exclaimed Chris. "What do you mean? Has Morrey or Serge said anything?"

"It is the one you call Morrey," Vari said. "Does he not understand the importance of this meeting?"

"Morrey! I'm sorry about that, Vari," Chris faltered. "I'm sure he didn't realize what he was saying. What did he say?"

"He said, 'Curse you, Vari, what have you done to my friends?' I understand his first words are an expression of hatred."

"He's probably very worried about not being able to speak to us," suggested Mervyn Williams. "Could we not send him a message to let him know we are all right?"

"No. Nor can I now let you leave this ship. The whole purpose of our meeting was to discover whether your people were yet ready to receive mine openly. I must see to what degree hatred and mistrust are still part of the human character. I must see how your friends will react."

"Are you going to keep us here?" Chris asked. "Are you holding us prisoners?"

"I am sorry this has happened, but I must be sure about you. It is necessary for you to remain in my ship so that I can assess the degree of hostility shown by your companions. You will be quite comfortable here, I assure you."

The astronauts felt the tingling that marked the change in their atomic structure. Without putting it to the test, they knew quite well that they would no longer be able to walk through the ship's wall. It was as if they were now confined in a cell without doors or windows.

Whatever Vari said, no matter what reason he gave, the plain fact was that they were prisoners. They were completely at the mercy of someone who had vastly more power than they. Chris had no doubt that Vari could destroy them in a twinkling if he so wished. Why, oh, why, had Morrey angered him?

"Would you like to relax and have something to eat?" Vari asked.

His tone was neither friendly or hostile, and Chris would have given a great deal to know what the alien was thinking.

"We are all feeling a little tired," he admitted, "so we'll accept your hospitality."

"Would you like to rest first or eat?"

"Eat," Tony burst out. Perhaps there was a slight twinkle in Vari's eye.

"Very well," he said. "Remain where you are. You can no longer follow me into the next room."

None of the six spoke at this reminder that they were prisoners. Their host—or jailer—disappeared through a section of the wall. While he was away, they went up to the shining dome for want of something better to do. While Tony examined it closely, the others gathered in an anxious little knot round Chris.

"How long do you think he'll keep us?" Colin Johnson asked in a low voice.

"I don't know," Chris answered in his normal tone. It

was no use to speak in whispers. If Vari had listening devices, they would be unimaginably sensitive. "His mission is to find out all he can about the human race. Until he's discovered how far Morrey's hostility will develop, I expect we shall stay as his guests."

As Chris finished speaking, Vari reappeared carrying a tray. On it were six bowls each containing a number of brown cubes about the size of a lump of sugar. Alongside each bowl was a pair of tongs, again like those used with sugar.

"Try this," Vari said, giving each a bowl and a pair of tongs, "and tell me what you think of it. This is my food."

Each of the astronauts took the proffered bowls, and Tony lost no time in trying one of the brown cubes. He chewed it with a doubtful expression.

"It's good!" he suddenly pronounced. "I like it."

By this time the others had tasted Vari's food. Chris found the brown substance, which he couldn't identify, quite appetizing. It tasted like a cross between a piece of steak and a lump of Christmas cake.

"What is this, Vari?" Mervyn asked the alien, who had been watching them curiously.

"It is a synthetic food which we use in my world. I am glad you like it. At least you did not think I would poison you."

Chris paused. He'd never even thought of the possibility, and neither had the others. Surely Vari could see that they trusted him. They had entered his ship freely and without hesitation. Perhaps he would overlook the intervention of Morrey.

It was a vain hope, for even as he watched his guests enjoying their unusual diet, Vari's face hardened again. With a sinking heart Chris guessed that he was picking up further messages from Morrey.

151

"Why don't you answer? Why don't you let Chris speak?" Morrey was shouting over his radio.

From Beta, Serge tried in vain to calm his friend. At last he put on his space suit and made his way toward Alpha. By the time he arrived Morrey was almost back into his suit.

"It's no use, Serge," the American thundered. "I'm going to blast my way into that monstrosity."

"Wait, Morrey, wait," pleaded Serge. "We've no proof that Chris and the others have come to harm. If you attack the alien ship, you could jeopardize their lives."

"If they are well, why doesn't Chris or the alien speak to us? How do we know that the ship won't lift off at any minute and Vari take his prisoners back as specimens to his own world? I'm sure the alien is picking up our radio. Why does he remain silent?"

"I don't know, but that's no reason for blasting his ship with a laser gun."

"Isn't it? I think it is, and I'm telling him so. He's only got to speak for me to call it off. Coming?"

"Yes, I'll come with you," Serge agreed, hoping that he would be able to restrain Morrey, who was making a final broadcast to the alien.

"Are you going to let me speak to Chris? If not, we're coming to blast our way into your ship!"

The radio remained stubbornly silent.

"Come on, Serge. Grab a gun," Morrey spat out.

Reluctantly the Russian took one of the laser guns from its rack. Though they would be useful in the unlikely event of attack by hostile life, their main function was to slice off rock samples for examination. Never, in all the expeditions that UNEXA had mounted, had a laser gun been used in anger. Until now.

For a moment the two astronauts paused at the foot of Alpha. The alien spaceship still lay brooding sullenly in

152

the distance. Then, with Morrey grimly in the lead, they set off toward it.

"Your friends are coming this way," Vari told his guests. "Morrey is demanding that I let you return."

"Well, aren't you going to let us?" Colin asked.

"Of course," Vari assured them. "But I must keep you here, as I have told you, to find out what your race will do under provocation. None of you will come to any harm."

"I hope you won't think too badly of Morrey," Chris said. "He must be worried sick about us. He would do anything to help us."

Vari looked at him coldly. Clearly he did not understand what Chris meant.

"Has he got a laser gun?" asked Colin.

"So I gather," Vari replied, "but have no fear. It cannot harm this ship. Nor will I do harm to your friends."

The six humans were extremely worried. They were distressed by the change in their relationship with Vari and even more anxious that Morrey and Serge shouldn't do anything foolish and provoke the alien to retaliate. Though Vari had promised not to harm them, there was no knowing what he might do if they used violence.

Outside, Morrey and Serge were plodding grimly toward the alien spaceship. In the light of the sun and of Uranus, the ship lay indifferently—insolently, it seemed—awaiting the approach of the Earthmen. Some twenty yards away from the foreign vessel, Morrey and Serge halted.

"For the last time, are you going to let our men out or at least speak to us?" demanded Morrey.

There was no response. Vari was silent. No astronauts appeared. Slowly, deliberately, Morrey raised his gun and aimed it at the nearest point of the ship. Then he pressed the button and set the shafts of searing light playing over the outer walls.

Nothing happened! The material of the alien spaceship was not fused, or even scorched; the laser beam appeared to have no effect whatsoever.

"You as well, Serge," Morrey yelled, and the Russian sent his beam to reinforce the other's.

Though the two guns concentrated on the same spot for almost half a minute, they hadn't the slightest effect on Vari's ship. Any metal or rock would have become molten and vaporized in far less time. At last the astronauts shut off their beams—defeated. Serge went up to the ship and examined the exact spot on which the two beams had concentrated. At least, he thought it was the spot. But there was nothing to distinguish it from its surroundings.

"Not even a scratch," he called out to Morrey, who was standing as if rooted to the ground. "Let's get back to the ship."

"Wait," Morrey snapped, suddenly galvanized into life. "Let's try somewhere else."

Serge agreed unwillingly and they blasted away at three more places around the ship. The result was the same. Nothing. At last Morrey agreed to return to Alpha.

As they walked back across the airless landscape, they were silent. Serge was wondering if Vari knew of their attack on him, what his reactions would be, and if it would affect their six friends. Perhaps they had been foolish in showing hostility to the alien. If Chris and the others had already been harmed—if they were dead—their action would have been useless anyhow. If Vari was restraining them for some reason, he might retaliate against his prisoners.

Morrey's thoughts were running along different lines. He was now more convinced than ever that the alien was evil and, with his amazing technology and fantastic materials, represented a threat to Earth. Already they had seen what Vari could do. If he and his fellows chose to land on Earth, they could become masters of the whole planet. This must be prevented. He, at least, would strike a blow for mankind.

Both astronauts returned to Morrey's ship. There seemed little point in separating in this hostile environment.

"There's nothing we can do but wait," Serge said, and sighed as they flung themselves on couches. It had been many hours since either had eaten, and though they didn't feel hungry, they knew that it was essential to keep up their calorie intake. They talked while Morrey grimly prepared a meal.

"The question is—how long should we wait?" the American said as he offered some food to his friend. "At what moment do we decide that the others are lost?"

"I wouldn't like to say," Serge answered. "They have been inside that ship for ten and a half hours. I don't think we can give up hope for a long time yet."

"But we can't sit here indefinitely and do nothing," Morrey exploded. "If everything is all right, why haven't they returned? Or even spoken to us? They must be wanting rest and food—if they're still alive! If this Vari creature wanted our goodwill, he would have let Chris and the others come back before now. No, Serge. I fear the worst. We are the only ones left."

Serge was beginning to think the same. Every silent minute that passed increased the likelihood that Morrey was right. Serge was rapidly coming to the conclusion that the only thing left for Morrey and him was to blast off and return to Earth. If they couldn't help their friends, their duty was to report to Control and to warn Earth about Vari and his race. This had been the main purpose of their expedition, to discover the source of the radio signals and to tell Control of their findings. Then UNEXA could prepare for the invasion by the aliens, which, sometime, must surely come.

So when Morrey suggested that they both prepare to take their ships off this hateful satellite, Serge agreed willingly. He did, however, insist on one final call to the alien. It had no effect.

"We might as well both be in Alpha," Serge observed. "It will make the takeoff easier."

The spaceship was built to be operated normally by a crew of four, and without the help of the Cape, the liftoff would be controlled manually, a really formidable task for only two men. So it was with some surprise that Serge listened to Morrey's objection.

"I know it would help for us to double up," he admitted. "But that means abandoning one of our ships. We mustn't leave anything behind that would help the alien find out more about us."

"But suppose Chris and the others did come out safely? They would have no means of getting back."

"If I thought there was the remotest chance of our friends still being alive, I wouldn't want to blast off at all," Morrey replied solemnly. "But I don't. Do you?"

Serge thought long and hard before he replied, but at last he decided that they must return to alert UNEXA.

"We go," he said simply.

"Then we take both ships," Morrey said briskly. "Do you think you can manage?"

Serge nodded silently. It would have been much better if they could have made the flight back to Earth together. The takeoff would have been simpler and the long journey back would not have been so lonely. But perhaps Morrey was right. They mustn't abandon either of the ships if it was possible to take them back to Earth.

Morrey breathed an inward sigh of relief that Serge had fallen in so easily with his plans. He couldn't let his friend know that only one ship would ever return to its base.

156

The other—his—would be utterly obliterated in destroying the alien and his vessel.

"Very well," Morrey forced himself to say calmly, "the sooner we are out of reach of that creature, the better."

"Do you think he will stop us blasting?" Serge asked.

"I don't know. We must risk it. Let's get started."

Serge began to put on his helmet, ready to cross to Beta. Morrey watched him affectionately, remembering that they were spending their last few minutes together. It was as much as he could do to appear calm.

"See you at the Cape," Serge grinned as he snapped his helmet into position and strode to the airlock.

"Good-bye," whispered Morrey as his friend disappeared.

19

"YOUR FRIENDS ARE ATTACKING my ship with their laser guns," Vari announced calmly. "As you see, they are completely ineffective. My ship is protected by a strong electrical field and your laser beams cannot penetrate it. Now they are withdrawing to your ships."

Chris felt like appealing once more to Vari to allow him to speak to Morrey and Serge. But a glance at the alien's stern, handsome features dissuaded him. Vari was intent on carrying out his tests of human reactions, and on the results would depend the decision whether or not the human race was yet ready for further contact.

Chris blamed himself for not having realized sooner that Morrey must be desperately anxious. He had been so carried away by the meeting with Vari that he had quite forgotten what Morrey must be feeling. He remembered now that Morrey had always seemed suspicious of Vari. That must have been why he had insisted on staying in Alpha. Chris wished that he had tried harder to persuade him to come and meet Vari. Now it was too late. Vari had evidently concluded from Morrey's actions that humans were distrustful and aggressive, and it seemed impossible to make him understand that Morrey was driven only by anxiety for his friends.

"Perhaps you will rest," Vari said.

It was as much a command as a suggestion, so Chris

nodded his agreement. All six astronauts had suddenly become very tired indeed.

"What can we rest upon?" asked Tony.

"Follow me," Vari said shortly, and he allowed the six to walk through the wall with him into another empty room.

"You may rest here," Vari said, his hand slipping down to his belt.

At once the astronauts felt weightless. Some field that Vari had set up had counteracted Ariel's weak gravity. They began to float just as they had done so many times during the long voyages through the solar system. But instead of drifting about the room as they would have done in their own spaceship, they hung steadily in one place. It was wonderfully comfortable, far better than lying in any bed, no matter how soft. Before long the six had drifted into sleep.

Morrey and Serge began their preparations. It would be a long and arduous task, one fraught with difficulties and dangers. Morrey had used this as an additional argument to persuade Serge to travel separately.

"It doubles the chances of one of us getting back to Earth," he'd pointed out mendaciously.

In the mind of each astronaut was the unspoken question: Would Vari permit them to escape? It would be easy for him to jam every electrical circuit in both ships. Would he?

"I can be ready in four hours," Serge radioed to Morrey.

"I'll be a little longer," the American replied untruthfully. "But you must blast off as soon as you can. I'll follow about an hour later."

"Shouldn't we lift off together?" Serge asked, puzzled.

"It would be safer to leave separately," Morrey told him. "I'll soon overtake you. Then we can make the ride together."

Of course, he had no intention of doing anything of the kind. He could have Alpha ready for liftoff in less than three hours, but he didn't want Serge to know this. Beta must be well away before he took Alpha up ready for the crash. If Serge had the remotest suspicion of what he was going to do, Morrey knew he would do all in his power to prevent it—even if he had to sit on top of the alien ship.

The astronauts exchanged a constant stream of conversation over their radios. So far there was not the slightest sign of interference from Vari. All the circuits were working perfectly. Instruments were tested and found to be all right. Valves and pumps operated correctly.

"Let's keep our fingers crossed," Morrey called to Serge. Even if Vari heard this, Morrey doubted whether he would know what the phrase meant.

There hadn't been the slightest move from the alien. If that monstrous ship hadn't been squatting menacingly a few yards away, the two anxious astronauts could have believed that Vari didn't exist. Except, of course, that he'd destroyed their six friends. With every minute that passed, every job completed successfully, their chance of escaping from his influence increased.

"I'm ready," a weary Serge reported at last.

"Fine. Then off you go," Morrey called back, striving to keep any quiver out of his voice. It would be the last message he would exchange with his friend, the last words he would utter to any human being. But he had no regrets. With all his heart he believed that his sacrifice would be worthwhile.

The orange flame that roared out of the base of Beta indicated that Serge hadn't detected anything amiss and had pressed his ignition switch. Morrey watched through his porthole with a full heart and raised a hand in farewell to the rapidly rising ship.

So Vari hadn't interfered in any way. No doubt he was

satisfied for the moment with his six victims. Morrey shuddered to think what might have happened to Chris and the others. He would avenge his friends and destroy the alien at the same time, and also postpone the conquest of Earth by Vari's race. If Serge succeeded in alerting UNEXA to the danger, maybe the conquest would be averted for ever.

Beta was now only a tiny speck of light in the black velvet sky. In a few more minutes it would be safe to take up Alpha ready for his attack.

"Chris! Colin! Robert! Mervyn! Norman! Tony!" he called for the last time over his radio, but, of course, there was no reply. Morrey gritted his teeth. Here goes. He pressed his ignition and felt the motors burst into life.

The barren landscape of Ariel began to fall away below him. As he gained speed and height, he looked down to see the shrinking alien spaceship. Then he shut off the motors but continued to rise under the ship's momentum. Though the satellite's gravity was low and though it was already more than twenty miles above the surface, Alpha would slowly come to a halt. In another ten minutes or so it would reach its maximum height. Then, as ever gathering speed, it would begin to fall back toward the surface from which it had come.

Morrey was tempted to make a call to Serge, partly to let him think that he, too, was on his way home, partly to test if Vari's barrage still prevented communication with Earth. Though he knew that any message he sent would reach Control only long after he was dead, he would have liked to say good-bye to the blue and green planet, the loveliest in the solar system, that was his home. But when he switched on, his radio was still dead. With a sigh Morrey turned to his panel of switches. He must turn the ship, reignite the motors, and aim for that hateful target, the alien ship.

Serge, too, had been waiting to see when he would be

beyond the belt of interference that Vari had set up. He kept his radio tuned ready to receive the first signals from Earth. All he heard was Morrey's last call-over of their lost friends' names. He knew Morrey would be feeling just as wretched as he did about the loss of their comrades. The sooner they could explain to Control what had happened, the better.

It didn't take long for Beta to reach escape velocity from Ariel. As soon as he'd reached it, Serge shut off his motors and was content to coast along. He'd wait for the arrival of Alpha alongside before building up speed for the homeward journey. How long would Morrey be? he wondered. It would be easy to find out by sending a call to his friend.

But it wasn't. Quite suddenly all the instruments and the radio went dead. Even the cabin light was almost extinguished. Frantically, Serge checked over circuit after circuit, to find nothing wrong. At last, sweating, he was forced to the conclusion that this was the work of the alien. Vari hadn't intended to let Morrey and him escape.

Unaware that Serge had been caught in the enemy's trap, Morrey completed the maneuver of turning his ship round. Then, viciously, he stabbed the ignition switch and began streaking back toward his hated target.

Within a few minutes, he knew, he would be dead, smashed in the violent impact he would soon be making. A wild exhilaration swept over him. It was a glorious way to die. He began to hum a tune.

How long Chris and the others had slept they didn't know. Suddenly, they were all awake, conscious that Vari was standing in their midst. A touch at his belt and the astronauts slid to the floor.

"What is it, Vari?" Chris asked, noting the hard expression on the alien's face.

162

"It is your friends," the alien replied. "They are leaving."

The news stunned the six. Leaving? That was impossible! Morrey and Serge would never desert them. It was unthinkable. Vari must be mistaken.

"What—what do you mean?" Norman Spier managed to gasp.

"From their conversation I gather that they believe you are dead. After they attacked my ship with what you call laser guns, they returned to your ships. Now both have lifted off and are presumably on the way back to Earth," Vari told his listeners calmly.

Chris didn't think for a moment that Vari was lying. If Morrey and Serge really believed that he and the others were dead, it would be the obvious action to take. Being unable to do anything more for their comrades, they were doing just what he would have wanted them to do—return and report. But he and his five friends were not dead. They were very much alive—and stranded on this lifeless satellite.

Vari was watching his guests more carefully than they knew as they tried to adjust themselves to their terrible situation. As their leader, Chris spoke for them all.

"Why didn't you let us speak to them?" he demanded. "They would have known, then, that we were all right. Now we are stranded in your ship. We cannot go home."

He had spoken calmly and without anger. Perhaps it was because he realized that anger would be misplaced. Perhaps he was too numbed to feel anger.

"Have no fear, my friends," Vari said. "Your comrades will not go far. I shall halt their ships in a little while, and then you can ask them to return for you."

"But how can you do that?" spluttered Tony.

The alien permitted himself to smile but didn't answer.

163

"Perhaps we could persuade Serge and Morrey to come and meet you," suggested Mervyn hopefully.

"That will not be necessary," Vari answered. "My mission is completed."

"You mean you have learned all you want to from us?" Chris asked.

"I believe so," the alien answered, "so I can now assist you to return to your home planet."

Chris would dearly have loved to ask Vari what was his opinion about humans, what his report would be to those who sent him. Had he decided that man was now ready for contact with other races? Or would the human race have to wait still longer?

While these questions were running through Chris's head, Vari left them, and immediately a hubbub broke out as the six astronauts began to discuss the situation urgently. Not one of them doubted Vari's ability to get their ships back to Ariel so that they could take off for Earth. How he would do it they didn't know. But then there was so much about the alien's technology that they didn't understand.

The six were talking together so earnestly that they didn't notice Vari's return until he spoke to them.

"I have more news for you, my friends," he told them. "I have halted one of your ships in flight. The other one has changed course. It is headed back here under power. I believe your friend Morrey intends to crash his ship on mine in order to destroy me."

What was there for them to say? The blinding tragedy of it all—the destruction of Vari, his ship, and themselves—was so unnecessary. If only Vari had allowed them to speak to Morrey and Serge. For the first time Chris found himself doubting the alien's wisdom. Certainly, from their point of view, he had made a colossal and tragic blunder.

164

While they were still reeling under the news, Vari spoke again.

"Tell me," he said—and his voice had a note of urgency —"why would your friend want to do this thing? Does he not realize that he himself will be destroyed?"

Chris thought carefully before he spoke. Somehow he realized that much depended on his answer.

"Morrey believes that you are evil and a danger to our planet," he said, choosing his words. "Remember, he doesn't know you as we do. But, believing that, and believing that you have harmed us, he must have felt it his duty to destroy you before you could do any more harm."

"Even if that meant destroying himself?" Vari asked.

"Of course," Chris answered. "We would all do the same." The other astronauts nodded.

Vari smiled. "At last I understand," he said. "I have learned something more about your race. You are more complex than I had realized. Now I will save this foolish but courageous young man." And he vanished once more from the room.

Beta was drifting along helplessly. Try as he could, Serge could bring no life back to any of the circuits. Neither could he reignite his motor. Suddenly he stopped floating without weight and was pressed to the floor as the ship gently accelerated. He rushed to a porthole and gazed in amazement. Beta was moving back to Ariel at an ever-increasing speed!

What was happening? His motors were dead, yet he was accelerating. He'd been traveling away from the satellite. Now he was rushing toward it. It could only be the work of the alien. Vari was somehow drawing him back to barren Ariel.

Meanwhile, what had happened to Morrey? Had the same fate befallen the American? Serge twisted his hands

165

in helpless agony. Within minutes now he, at least, would crash on the rocky surface. Before that, would he see the smoking wreck of Alpha marking the death spot of his last surviving friend?

Morrey's exhilaration had mounted with his speed. His end would be quick and glorious. It would come in one blinding, searing crash onto the ugly spaceship. Surely not even that evil monster and its alien master would be able to withstand the stupendous impact. Alpha and its heroic pilot rushed on to its inevitable doom.

20

IN SPITE OF HIS TRAINING, Morrey nevertheless fainted as his ship decelerated at an incredible speed. Alpha, its engines dead, was rapidly slowing down under the influence of an antigravity beam from Vari. For, just as Vari's civilization could propel ships by means of a concentrated gravity beam, so, too, it had mastered the technique of using antigravity to repel. Morrey's ship was in the center of such a force.

Morrey was still unconscious as Alpha settled gently a few hundred yards from its original position. Almost at the same time Beta, too, touched down, with the incredulous and helpless Serge watching the whole operation. Vari had had to apply far less power to Beta than had been needed to counteract Alpha's headlong flight. By the time Morrey had recovered, even the dust had settled, and except that they were in slightly different places, it was as though the two ships had never moved.

"Go out now and meet your friends," Vari told his six guests. "If you wish, I will come with you."

"Oh, do, please," Tony said eagerly. "We'd like you to meet Morrey and Serge."

"Perhaps they will not wish to meet me," Vari said with a twinkle.

"I think everything can be explained," said Chris.

It was a joyous party that set out from Vari's ship. Serge

and Morrey were only just recovering from their experiences when they each saw an unbelievable sight. From their portholes they saw a number of space-suited figures emerge from the alien vessel and begin to walk toward them. Several times Morrey counted their number before he could believe his senses. There were *seven* people coming toward the two ships from Earth, and the seventh was much taller than the others!

Long before the seven had crossed even halfway toward Alpha and Beta, there had been an almost incoherent babble across the radios. At last Chris had managed to convey to his remaining two friends that all was well, that Vari had not harmed them in any way.

"We're bringing him to meet you," he concluded, "and then you can see for yourselves. Shall we all meet in Alpha?"

Before Morrey had had time to collect himself, Chris was leading his party up the ladder, and Serge joined them. And off came all the helmets.

"Morrey and Serge, this is Vari," Chris burst out as soon as he could speak.

For a moment Morrey stood irresolute, silent. It was the alien who spoke first.

"I think you are a very brave young man," he said simply.

Morrey flushed and held out his hand. Suddenly he knew that he had been wrong from the start about the visitor from space.

Chris and the rest were all eager to describe the fantastic things that they had seen and heard inside the alien ship. Chris took particular care to explain why Vari hadn't let them communicate and why he'd put up a barrage to stop messages to and from Earth.

Vari waited for the six humans to finish talking before he spoke.

168

"My friends—and I hope we are now all friends—you know the purpose of our meeting. I was sent to assess the development of humans so that my people could decide whether we should yet establish final contact. A plan was devised to bring you to this remote satellite where we could meet and talk. Now I must return to my own world and let you go back to yours."

"And what will you tell your people?" Chris asked quietly.

"That the human race is not ready for our meeting. That we must postpone our contact once again," Vari replied.

"Then—then we've let our folks down?" Morrey murmured.

"Not at all," the alien reassured them. "I have analyzed you more deeply than you know. You are still fairly primitive creatures. You experience distrust, hatred, and fear. But you have inquiring minds and display great courage and a sense of duty."

"So you will make contact with us sometime?" Tony asked.

"That is not for me to decide. But I believe we shall," Vari told him. "When that will be, I do not know. You have to evolve a little further yet."

"But we can tell our people all about you and urge them forward," Norman declared.

"No, my friends, that you cannot do," Vari told them. "Your race must know nothing of our encounter. I shall expunge all memory of what has happened from your minds."

"But we have seen you. Our people have received your signals. They know that someone intelligent has sent them," Mervyn pointed out.

"That is true. But I shall be gone before you depart, and you will only remember having seen a strange shape that suddenly disappeared. This is all your people will learn from you, so they will still not be quite certain about my signals."

"Can't we take back any technical information? It would help us a lot," pleaded Tony.

"No. You will discover all you need to know in good time. It would be harmful for you to learn too much too quickly. You are not yet using all the discoveries you have made to the best advantage of your race," Vari replied.

"But won't your people come to visit us at all?" Robert Campbell asked.

"Oh, indeed we shall," Vari smiled. "We shall come among you whenever we judge that you need a little nudge forward. You will not recognize us, of course. You will think of us as just outstanding members of your race."

There seemed little else to say. The alien had decreed that his people and man must still go their separate ways. Chris and his companions could only accept that decision. The sadness of it all was, however, tinged with hope that—some day—the races would meet again, that man would have earned the privilege of becoming friends with Vari and his like.

"Good-bye, my friends," the alien said with a kindly smile. "I must return to my world and you to yours. But perhaps at some time in the future, such a parting will not be necessary. Meanwhile, I bid you all farewell."

One by one the astronauts shook Vari's outstretched hand. When the farewells were over, Vari replaced his helmet and squeezed through Alpha's airlock. The astronauts crowded round the portholes to watch him on his way. None of them spoke. As he reached his ship, Vari paused, turned round, and waved. Though they knew he couldn't see them, they all waved back. A moment later Vari had disappeared into his ship—gone forever from the sight of human eye.

"Well," sighed Chris, "the sooner we are on our way

back, the better. Let's have a last meal together before we divide up. Colin, fetch out the best we have."

And so the eight young men ate an appetizing meal. It began quietly enough and then, gradually, their spirits rose as they looked forward to the journey home. Voices rose, conversation became louder, excitement grew. Then, suddenly, for no more than a fraction of a second, the hubbub ceased. Perhaps few of the eight even noticed the break.

"Hey! It's gone!"

It was Tony who had called out. By chance he had glanced through one of the portholes in the direction of the strange shape they had decided was their objective. Immediately the others crowded round.

Where the peculiar structure had rested, and from where the intriguing radio signals had come was a barren space. It was as if the alien ship—if that is what it had been—had never existed. Chris could have beaten his head against the cabin walls in anguish at the thought that the astronauts had been wasting their time. They had been celebrating their safe landing and the end of their long separation by an informal party aboard Alpha. Why, oh, why, hadn't they gone immediately to explore the strange shape they had come so far to see?

Now it was too late. They would never know whether it was really a spaceship, and whether it housed some creature from outer space. It certainly hadn't looked like a spaceship. But it had been there when they landed, and now it had vanished. Yet they had felt no vibration whatsoever. If it had been a ship, Chris would have expected Alpha to have shuddered as the vast structure blasted off. It was inconceivable that any vessel could just slip away unnoticed.

"Let's have a look," suggested Morrey, and the astronauts lost no time in following his suggestion. They hurried to the spot where they believed the alien spaceship had been, but because there wasn't the slightest sign to

171

distinguish it from any other on the barren satellite, they couldn't be quite sure.

"No blast marks, no displaced rocks," Norman Spier observed.

Try as they would, they couldn't find a single sign that anything unusual had ever been there.

"We haven't imagined it, have we?" asked the astounded Mervyn.

Chris regretted that they hadn't photographed the outlandish thing, if only to settle whether or not it had ever existed. Control would want to know what they had found at the end of their long voyage. They would wish to hear if any explanation had been found for the unsettling radio signals that had made the expedition necessary.

What would they say? Confess that they had failed to make any observations on the alien object? Try to give a verbal description of it? Even as they stood together uncertainly, the memory of the object was fading rapidly. They soon began to disagree about its size, shape, and appearance.

"Let's get back," Chris suggested wearily. There was little point in staying on Ariel any longer. It seemed unlikely that they would discover where the radio signals came from. Perhaps, after all, there was some natural source. Even if they had originated from the strange object that had now disappeared, the explorers could offer no explanation. Rather despondently, they trooped back to their respective ships.

"We're lifting off in one hour," Chris reported to Control. They would be well on their way before the Cape received this information.

"Control calling Uranus Alpha and Beta. We are still not getting any signals," a distant voice crackled out monotonously every few minutes.

"Must be due to some local interference," Tony muttered as he completed the check on their own instruments.

172

As the two ships began their long journey back to Earth, Chris settled into his couch. Now he had time to reflect, he found he was a little hazy about some of the things that had happened recently. For example, he wasn't quite sure just how long they had spent on the satellite. The electrical interference that had cut off their communication with Control must also have affected other instruments such as the chronometer.

Had there really been a strange spaceship on Ariel? He could scarcely recall the object's outlines. Certainly from what he remembered, it couldn't have been a ship. It had no sign of rocket motors, or even an aerodynamic shape. He was very, very tired and looked forward to a long sleep. Around him his companions already slumbered, and he knew that in Beta things were the same. Gratefully, he closed his eyes.

Then followed the long journey home, with extensive spells of hypothermia and short periods of activity in between. Gradually the time lag between a message and its answer grew less as the ships passed inside the orbits of Saturn, Jupiter, and Mars. At last the crews were aroused from their frozen sleep for the last time. From now on they must be alert to guide their ships over the last few million miles.

Excitement naturally was growing. Whiskers had remained at the Cape and had resumed his old role of exchanging banter with the incoming crews. Sir Billy and Lord Benson were also settled in to await their arrival. Chris particularly was glad that his old chief would be at Control when they landed.

Now the last hours had come. First Alpha and then Beta transferred to earth orbit. The final calculations were made on the giant computer at Control. The last orders were issued, and the two ships began their glide back to Earth. The touchdown went without incident.

After a quick medical checkup of the crews, there began

the usual embraces and back slapping. It was good to be back on dear old Earth once more and to be with one's friends again! Lord Benson and Sir Billy seemed just a little older to the astronauts, but they had to remember that they had been in space for many long months. Whiskers roared his welcome in an effort to conceal his own emotion at the safe return of his friends.

After calmness was at last restored, after the travelers had bathed and eaten a hearty meal, the first debriefing session was held.

It was a disappointing affair. Somehow, Chris felt that he was letting the side down because he could give so little positive information. No, they hadn't met any beings from another world. No, they hadn't seen an alien spaceship, unless that strange, ungainly shape had been one. The vagueness of all their descriptions of it led their questioners to believe that the very sight of it might have been an hallucination coming at the end of a long and trying journey. No, they were unable to account for the radio signals that had seemed to come from another intelligence.

Man, it seemed, must still wait for his first contact with people from other worlds. It was a great disappointment that the expedition had been unable to bring back positive proof of their existence.

"We were only on Ariel for just over eight hours," Chris apologized, "but I'm sure that if we'd been there for eight weeks, we wouldn't have returned any wiser."

A strange look had come over Sir Billy Gillanders' face. Without speaking he scribbled a message and passed the pad to Lord Benson. Benson looked down at what his friend had written.

"They were on Ariel for over three days," it said.